SEDUCTION OF THE MINOTAUR

SEDUCTION
of the MINOTAUR

Anaïs Nin

Afterword by Wayne McEvilly

SWALLOW PRESS/OHIO UNIVERSITY PRESS
ATHENS

Printed in the United States of America

05 04 03 02 01 00   9 8 7 6

Swallow Press / Ohio University Press books
are printed on acid-free paper ∞

This book is printed on recycled paper

Cover photo from original painting by Jean Varda

Library of Congress Cataloging-in-Publication Data
Nin, Anais, 1903-1977.
        Seduction of the Minotaur / by Anais Nin :
afterword by Wayne McEvilly.
        p.   cm.
        ISBN 0-8040-0268-1
        I. Title.
PS3527. I865S4   1989
813'.52 – dc 20   89–21906
                                        CIP

Some voyages have their inception in the blueprint of a dream, some in the urgency of contradicting a dream. Lillian's recurrent dream of a ship that could not reach the water, that sailed laboriously, pushed by her with great effort, through city streets, had determined her course toward the sea, as if she would give this ship, once and for all, its proper sea bed.

She had landed in the city of Golconda, where the sun painted everything with gold, the lining of her thoughts, the worn valises, the plain beetles, Golconda of the golden age, the golden aster, the golden eagle, the golden goose, the golden fleece, the golden robin, the goldenrod, the goldenseal, the golden warbler, the golden wattles, the golden wedding, and the gold fish, and the gold of pleasure, the goldstone, the gold thread, the fool's gold.

With her first swallow of air she inhaled a drug of forgetfulness well known to adventurers.

Tropic, from the Greek, signified change and turning.

So she changed and turned, and was metamorphosed by the light and caressing heat into a spool of silk. Every movement she made from that moment on, even the carrying of her valise, was softened and pleasurable. Her nerves, of which she had always been sharply aware, had become instead strands from a spool of silk, spiraling through the muscles.

"How long do you intend to stay?" asked the official. "How much money do you carry with you? In what currency? Do you have a return ticket?"

You had to account for every move, arrival or exit. In the world there was a conspiracy against improvisation. It was only permitted in jazz.

The guitars and the singing opened fire. Her skin blossomed and breathed. A heavy wave of perfume came down the jungle on the right, and a fine spray of waves came from the left. On the beach the natives swung in hammocks of reeds. The tender Mexican voices sang love songs which cradled and rocked the body as did the hammocks.

Where she came from only jewels were placed in satin-lined cushioned boxes, but here it was thoughts and memories which the air, the scents, and the music conspired to hypnotize by softness.

But the airport official who asked cactus-pointed questions wore no shirt, nor did the porters, so that Lillian decided to be polite to the smoothest torso and show respect only to the strongest muscle.

The absence of uniforms restored the dignity and importance of the body. They all looked untamed and free, in their bare feet, as if they had assumed the duties of receiving the travelers only temporarily and would soon return to their hammocks, to swimming and singing. Work was one of the absurdities of existence. Don't you think so, Senorita? said their laughing eyes while they appraised her from head to toes. They looked at her openly, intently, as children and animals do, with a physical vision, measuring only physical attributes, charm, aliveness, and not titles, possessions, or

6

occupations. Their full, complete smile was not always answered by the foreigners, who blinked at such sudden warmth of smile as they did at the dazzling sun. Against the sun they wore dark glasses, but against these smiles and open naked glances they could only defend their privacy with a half-smile. Not Lillian. Her very full, rounded lips had always given such a smile. She could respond to this naked curiosity, naked interest, proximity. Thus animals and childen stare, with their whole, concentrated attentiveness. The natives had not yet learned from the white man his inventions for traveling away from the present, his scientific capacity for analyzing warmth into a chemical substance, for abstracting human beings into symbols. The white man had invented glasses which made objects too near or too far, cameras, telescopes, spyglasses, objects which put glass between living and vision. It was the image he sought to possess, not the texture, the living warmth, the human closeness.

The natives saw only the present. This communion of eyes and smiles was elating. Where Lillian came from people seemed intent on not seeing each other. Only children looked at her with this unashamed curiosity. Poor white man, wandering and lost in his proud possession of a dimension in which bodies became invisible to the naked eye, as if staring were an immodest act. Already she felt incarnated, in full possession of her own body because the porter was in full possession of his, and this concentration upon the present allowed no interruption or short circuits of the physical contact. When she turned away from the porter it was to find a smiling taxi driver who seemed to be saying: "I am not keen on going anywhere. It is just as good right here, right now . . . ."

He was scratching his luxuriant black hair, and he carried his wet bathing suit around his neck.

The guitars kept up their musical fire. The beggars squatted around the airport. Blind or crippled, they smiled.

7

The festivities of nature bathed them in gold and anesthetized their suffering.

Clothes seemed ponderous and superfluous in the city of Golconda.

Golconda was Lillian's private name for this city which she wanted to rescue from the tourist-office posters and propaganda. Each one of us possesses in himself a separate and distinct city, a unique city, as we possess different aspects of the same person. She could not bear to love a city which thousands believed they knew intimately. Golconda was hers. True, it had been at first a pearl-fishing village. True, a Japanese ship had been wrecked here, slave ships had brought Africans, other ships delivered spices, and Spanish ships had brought the art of filigree, of lace making. A shipwrecked Spanish galley had scattered on the beach baptism dresses which the women of southern Mexico had adopted as headgear.

The legend was that when the Japanese pearl divers had been driven away they had destroyed the pearl caches, and Golconda became a simple fishing village. Then the artists had come on donkeys, and discovered the beauty of the place. They had been followed by the real-estate men and hotelkeepers. But none could destroy Golconda. Golconda remained a city where the wind was like velvet, where the sun was made of radium, and the sea as warm as a mother's womb.

The porters were deserting before all the baggage was distributed. They had earned enough, just enough for the day for food, beer, a swim, and enough to take a girl dancing, and they did not want any more. So the little boys of ten and twelve, who had been waiting for this opening, were seeking to carry bags bigger than themselves.

The taxi driver, who was in no hurry to go anywhere in his dilapidated car, saw his car filling up, and decided it was time to put on his clean laundry-blue shirt.

The three men who were to share the taxi with Lillian

8

were already installed. Perhaps because they were in city clothes or perhaps because they were not smiling, they seemed to be the only subjects the sun could not illumine. The sea's aluminum reflectors had even penetrated the old taxi and found among the cracked leather some stuffing which had come out of the seat and which the sun transformed into angel hair such as grows on Christmas trees.

One of the men helped her into the car and introduced himself with Spanish colonial courtesy: "I am Doctor Hernandez."

He had the broad face she had seen in Mayan sculpture, the round high cheekbones, the aquiline nose, the full mouth slanting downward while the eyes slanted upward. His skin was a light olive which came from the mixture of Indian and Spanish blood. His smile was like the natives', open and total, but it came less often and faded quickly, leaving a shadow over his face.

She looked out the window to explore her new territory of pleasure. Everything was novel. The green of the foliage was not like any other greens: it was deeper, lacquered, and moist. The leaves were heavier, fuller, the flowers bigger. They seemed surcharged with sap, and more alive, as if they never had to close against the frost, or even a colder night. As if they had no need of sleep.

The huts made of palm leaves recalled Africa. Some were pointed on top and on stilts. Others had slanting roofs, and the palm leaves extended far enough to create shadows all around the house.

The lagoon on the left of the road showed a silver surface which sometimes turned to sepia. It was half filled with floating lagoon flowers. Trees and bushes seemed like new vegetation, also on stilts, dipping twisted roots into the water as the reeds dipped their straight and flexible roots. Herons stood on one leg. Iguanas slithered away, and parrots became hysterically gay.

Lillian's eyes returned to the Doctor. His thoughts were

9

elsewhere, so she looked at the American who had introduced himself as Hatcher. He was an enginer who had come to Mexico years before to build roads and bridges, and had remained and married a Mexican woman. He spoke perfect Spanish, and was a leathery-skinned man who had been baked by the sun as dark as the natives. The tropics had not relaxed his forward-jutting jaw and shoulders. He looked rigid, lean, hard-fleshed. His bare feet were in Mexican sandals, the soles made of discarded rubber tires. His shirt was open at the neck. But on him the negligent attire still seemed a uniform to conquer, rather than a way of submitting to, the tropics.

"Golconda may seem beautiful to you, but it's spoiled by tourism. I found a more beautiful place farther on. I had to hack my way to it. I have a beach where the sand is so white it hurts the eyes like a snow slope. I'm building a house. I come to Golconda once a week to shop. I have a jeep. If you like you can drive out with me for a visit. Unless, like most Americans, you have come here to drink and dance. . . ."

"I'm not free to drink and dance. I have to play every night with the jazz orchestra."

"Then you must be Lillian Beye," said the passenger who had not yet spoken. He was a tall blond Austrian who spoke a harsh Spanish but with authority. "Im the owner of the Black Pearl. I engaged you."

"Mr. Hansen?"

He shook her hand without smiling. He was fair-skinned. The tropics had not been able to warm him, or to melt the icicle-blue eyes.

Lillian felt that these three men were somehow interfering with her own tasting of Golconda. They semed intent on giving her an image of Golconda she did not want. The Doctor wanted her to notice only that the children were in need of care, the American wanted her to recoil from tour-

10

ism, and the owner of the Black Pearl made the place seem like a night club.

The taxi stopped for gasoline. An enormously fat American, unshaved for many days, rose from a hammock to wait on them.

"Hello, Sam," said Doctor Hernandez. "How is Maria? You didn't bring her to me for her injection."

Sam shouted to a woman dimly visible inside the palm-leaf shack. She came to the door. Her long black shawl was fastened to her shoulders and her baby was cradled in the folds of it as if inside a hammock.

Sam repeated the Doctor's question. She shrugged her shoulders: "No time," she said and called: "Maria!"

Maria came forward from a group of children, carrying a boat made out of a cocoanut shell. She was small for her age, delicately molded, like a miniature child, as Mexican children often are. In the eyes of most Mexican painters, these finely chiseled beings with small hands and feet and slender necks and waists become larger than nature, with the sinews and muscles of giants. Lillian saw them tender and fragile and neat. The Doctor saw them ill.

The engineer said to Lillian: "Sam was sent here twenty years ago to build bridges and roads. He married a native. He does nothing but sleep and drink."

"It's the tropics," said Hansen.

"You've never been to the Bowery," said Lillian.

"But in the tropics all white men fall apart. . ."

"I've heard that but I never believed it. Any more than I believe all adventurers are doomed. I think such beliefs are merely an expression of fear, fear of expatriation, fear of adventure."

"I agree with you," said the Doctor. "The white man who falls apart in the tropics is the same one who would fall apart anywhere. But in foreign lands they stand out more because they are few, and we notice them more."

11

"And then at home, if you want to fall apart, there are so many people to stop you. Relatives and friends foil your attempts! You get sermons, lectures, threats, and you are even rescued."

The Austrian laughed: "I can't help thinking how much encouragement you would get here."

"You, Mr. Hatcher, didn't disintegrate in the tropics!"

Hatcher answered solemnly: "But I am a happy man. I have succeeded in living and feeling like a native."

"Is that the secret, then? It's those who don't succeed in going native, in belonging, who get desperately lonely and self-destructive?"

"Perhaps," said the Doctor pensively. "It may also be that you Americans are work-cultists, and work is the structure that holds you up, not the joy of pure living."

His words were accompanied by a guitar. As soon as one guitar moved away, the sound of another took its place, to continue this net of music that would catch and maintain you in flight from sadness, suspended in a realm of festivities.

Just as every tree carried giant brilliant flowers playing chromatic scales, runs and trills of reds and blues, so the people vied with them in wearing more intense indigoes, more flaming oranges, more platinous whites, or else colors which resembled the purple insides of mangoes, the flesh tones of pomegranates.

The houses were covered with vines bearing bell-shaped flowers playing coloraturas. The guitars inside of the houses or on the doorsteps took up the color chromatics and emitted sounds which evoked the flavor of guava, papaya, cactus figs, anise, saffron, and red pepper.

Big terra-cotta jars, heavily loaded donkeys, lean and hungry dogs, all recalled images from the Bible. The houses were all open; Lillian could see babies asleep in hammocks, holy pictures on the white stucco walls, old people on rocking chairs, and photographs of relatives pinned on the walls together with old palm leaves from the Palm Sunday feast.

12

The sun was setting ostentatiously, with all the pomp of embroidered silks and orange tapestries of Oriental spectacles. The palms had a naked elegance, and wore their giant plumes like languid feather dusters sweeping the tropical sky of all clouds, keeping it as transparent as a sea.shell.

Restaurants served dinner out in the open. On one long communal table was a bowl of fish soup and fried fish. Inside the houses people had begun to light the oil lamps which had a more vivacious flicker than candles.

The Doctor had been talking about illness. "Fifteen years ago this place was actually dangerous. We had malaria, dysentery, elephantiasis, and other illnesses you would not even know about. They had no hospital and no doctor until I came. I had to fight dysentery alone, and teach them not to sleep in the same bed with their farm animals."

"How did you happen to come here?"

"We have a system in Mexico. Before obtaining their degrees, young medical students have to have a year of practice in whatever small town needs them. When I first came here I was only eighteen. I was irresponsible, and a bit sullen at having to take care of fishermen who could neither read nor write nor follow instructions of any kind. When I was not needed, I read French novels and dreamed of the life in large cities which I was missing. But gradually I came to love my fishermen, and when the year was over I chose to stay."

The eyes of the people were full of burning life. They squatted like Orientals next to their wide flat baskets filled with fruits and vegetables. The fruit was not piled negligently but arranged in a careful Persian design of decorative harmonies. Strings of chili hung from the rafters, chili to wake them from their dreams, dreams born of scents and rhythms, and the warmth that fell from the sky like the fleeciest blanket. Even the twilight came without a change of temperature or alteration in the softness of the air.

It was not only the music from the guitars but the music of the body that Lillian heard—a continuous rhythm of life. There was a rhythm in the way the women lifted the water jugs onto their heads, and walked balancing them. There was a rhythm in the way the shepherds walked after their lambs and their cows. It was not just the climate, but the people themselves who exuded a more ardent life.

Hansen was looking out the taxi window with a detached and bored expression. He did not see the people. He did not notice the children who, because of their black hair cut in square bangs and their slanted eyes, sometimes looked like Japanese. He questioned Lillian on entertainers. What entertainers from New York or Paris or London should he bring to the Black Pearl?

The hotel was at the top of the hill, one main building and a cluster of small cottages hidden by olive trees and cactus. It faced the sea at a place where huge boiling waves were trapped by crevices in the rocks and struck at their prison with cannon reverberations. Two narrow gorges were each time assaulted, the waves sending foam high in the air and leaping up as if in a fury at being restrained.

The receptionist at the desk was dressed in rose silk, as if registering guests and handing out keys were part of the festivities. The manager came out, holding out his hand paternally, as though his immense bulk conferred on him a patriarchy, and said: "You are free to enjoy yourself tonight. You won't have to start playing until tomorrow night. Did you see the posters?"

He led her to the entrance where her photograph, enlarged, faced her like the image of a total stranger. She never recognized herself in publicity photographs. I look pickled, she thought.

A dance was going on, on the leveled portion of the rock beside the hotel. The music was intermittent, for the wind carried some of the notes away, and the sound of the sea absorbed others, so that these fragments of mambos had an abstract distinction like the music of Erik-Satie. It also made the couples seem to be dancing sometimes in obedience to it, and sometimes in obedience to the gravitations of their secret attractions.

A barefoot boy carried Lillian's bags along winding paths. Flowers brushed her face as she passed. Both music and sea sounds grew fainter as they climbed. Cottages were set capriciously on rock ledges, hidden by reeds, or camouflaged in bougainvillaea. The boy stopped before a cottage with a palm-leaf roof.

In front of it was a long tile terrace, with a hemp hammock strung across it. The room inside had whitewashed walls, and contained only a bed, a table, and a chair. Parasoling over the cottage was a giant tree which bore leaves shaped like fans. The encounter of the setting sun and rising moon had combined to paint everything in the changing colors of mercury.

As Lillian opened a bureau drawer, a mouse that had been making a nest of magnolia petals suddenly fled.

She showered and dressed hastily, feeling that perhaps the beauty and velvety softness of the night might not last, that if she delayed it would change to coldness and harshness. She put on the only dress she had that matched the bright flowers, an orange cotton. Then she opened the screen door. The night lay unchanged, serene, filled with tropical whisperings, as if leaves, birds, and sea breezes possessed musicalities unknown to northern countries, as if the richness of the scents kept them all intently alive.

The tiles under her bare feet were warm. The perfume she had sprayed on herself evaporated before the stronger perfumes of carnation and honeysuckle.

She walked back to the wide terrace where people sat on deck chairs waiting for each other and for dinner.

The expanse of sky was like an infinite canvas on which human beings were incapable of projecting images from their human life because they would seem out of scale and absurd.

Lillian felt that nature was so powerful it absorbed her into itself. It was a drug for forgetting. People seemed warmer and nearer, as the stars seemed nearer and the moon warmer.

The sea's orchestration carried away half the spoken words and made talking and laughing seem a mere casual accompaniment, like the sound of birds. Words had no weight. The intensity of the colors made them float in space like balloons, and the velvet texture of the climate gave them a purely decorative quality like other flowers. They had no abstract meaning, being received by the senses which only recognized touch, smell, and vision, so that these people sitting in their chairs became a part of a vivid animated mural. A brown shoulder emerging from a white dress, the limpidity of a smile in a tanned face, the muscular tension of a brown leg, seemed more eloquent than the voices.

This is an exaggerated spectacle, thought Lillian, and it makes me comfortable. I was always an exaggerated character because I was trying to create all by myself a climate which suited me, bigger flowers, warmer words, more fervent relationships, but here nature does it for me, creates the climate I need within myself, and I can be languid and at rest. It is a drug . . . a drug . . .

Why were so many people fearful of the tropics? "All adventurers came to grief." Perhaps they had not been able to make the transition, to alchemize the life of the mind into the life of the senses. They died when their minds were overpowered by nature, yet they did not hesitate to dilute it in alcohol.

Even while Golconda lulled her, she was aware of several mysteries entering her reverie. One she called the sorrows of Doctor Hernandez. The other was why do exiles come to a bad end (if they did, of which she was not sure). From where she sat, she saw the Doctor arrive with his pro-

16

fessional valise. But this burden he deposited at the hotel desk, and then he walked toward Lillian as if he had been seeking her.

"You haven't had dinner yet? Come and have it with me. We'll have it in the Black Pearl, so you will become familiar with the place where you are going to play every night."

The Black Pearl had been built of driftwood. It was a series of terraces overhanging the sea. Red ship lanterns illumined a jazz band playing for a few dancers.

Because the hiss of the sea carried away some of the overtones, the main drum beat seemed more emphatic, like a giant heart pulsing. The more volatile cadences, the ironic notes, the lyrical half-sobs of the trombone rose like sea spray and were lost. As if the instrumentalists knew this, they repeated their climbs up invisible antennae into vast spaces of volatile joys and shrank the sorrows by speed and flight, decanting all the essences, and leaving always at the bottom the blood beat of the drums.

The Doctor was watching her face. "Did I frighten you with all my talk about sickness?"

"No, Doctor Hernandez, illness does not frighten me. Not physical illness. The one that does is unknown in Golconda. And I'm a convalescent. And in any case, it's one which does not inspire sympathy."

Her words had been spoken lightly, but they caused the Doctor's smooth face to wrinkle with anxiety. Anxiety? Fear? She could not read his face. It had the Indian sculptural immobility. Even when the skin wrinkled with some spasm of pain, the eyes revealed nothing, and the mouth was not altered.

She felt compelled to ask: "Are you unhappy? Are you in trouble?"

She knew it was dangerous to question those who were accustomed to doing the questioning, to being depended on (and well did Lillian know that those who were in the posi-

17

tion of consolers, guides, healers, felt uncomfortable in any reversal) but she took the risk.

He answered, laughing: "No, I'm not, but if being unhappy would arouse your interest, I'm willing to be. It was tactless of me to speak of illness in this place created for pleasure. I nearly spoiled *your* pleasure. And I can see you are one who has not had too much of it, one of the underprivileged of pleasure! Those who have too much nauseate me. I don't know why. I'm glad when they get dysentery or serious sunburns. It is as if I believed in an even distribution of pleasure. Now you, for instance, have a right to some . . . not having had very much."

"I didn't realize it was so apparent."

"It is not so apparent. Permit me to say I am unusually astute. Diagnostic habit. You *appear* free and undamaged, vital and without wounds."

"Diagnostic clairvoyance, then?"

"Yes. But here comes our professional purveyor of pleasure. He may be more beneficent for you."

Hansen sat down beside them, and began to draw on the tablecloth. "I'm going to add another terrace, then I will floodlight the trees and the divers. I will also have a light around the statue of the Virgin so that everyone can see the boys praying before they dive." His glance was cold, managerial. The sea, the night, the divers were all in his eyes, properties of the night club. The ancient custom of praying before diving one hundred feet into a narrow rocky gorge was going to become a part of the entertainment.

Lillian turned her face away from him, and listened to the jazz.

Jazz was the music of the body. The breath came through aluminum and copper tubes, it was the body's breath, and the strings' wails and moans were echoes of the body's music. It was the body's vibrations which rippled from the fingers. And the mystery of the withheld theme known to the musicians alone was like the mystery of our secret life. We give to others only peripheral improvisations. The plots and themes of the music like the plots and themes of our life never alchemized into words, existed only in a state of music, stirring or numbing, exalting or despairing, but never named.

When she turned her face unwillingly towards Hansen, he was gone, and then she looked at the Doctor and said: "This is a drugging place. . . ."

"There are so many kinds of drugs. One for remembering and one for forgetting. Golconda is for forgetting. But it is not a permanent forgetting. We may seem to forget a person, a place, a state of being, a past life, but meanwhile what we are doing is selecting a new cast for the reproduction of the same drama, seeking the closest reproduction to the friend, the lover, or the husband we are striving to forget. And one day we open our eyes, and there we are caught in the same pattern, repeating the same story. How could it be otherwise? The design comes from within us. It is internal."

There were tears in Lillian's eyes, for having made friends immediately not with a new, a beautiful, a drugging place, but with a man intent on penetrating the mysteries of the human labyrinth from which she was a fugitive. She was almost angered by his persistence. A man should respect one's desire to have no past. But even more damaging was his conviction that we live by a series of repetitions until the experience is solved, understood, liquidated . . . .

"You will never rest until you have discovered the familiar within the unfamiliar. You will go around as these tourists do, searching for flavors which remind you of home, begging for Coca-Cola instead of tequila, cereal foods instead of papaya. Then the drug will wear off. You will discover that barring a few divergences in skin tone, or mores, or language, you are still related to the same kind of person because it all comes from within you, you are the one fabricating the web."

19

Other people were dancing around them, so obedient to the rhythms that they seemed like algae in the water, welded to each other, and swaying, the colored skirts billowing, the white suits like frames to support the flower arrangements made by the women's dresses, their hair, their jewels, their lacquered nails. The wind sought to carry them away from the orchestra, but they remained in its encirclement of sound like Japanese kites moved by strings from the instruments.

Lillian asked for another drink. But as she drank it, she knew that one of the drops of the Doctor's clairvoyance had fallen into her glass, that a part of what he had said was already proved true. The first friend she had made in Golconda, choosing him in preference to the engineer and the night-club manager, resembled, at least in his role, a personage she had known who was nicknamed "The Lie Detector"; for many months this man had lived among a group of artists extracting complete confessions from them without effort and subtly changing the course of their lives.

Not to yield to the Doctor's challenge, she brusquely turned the spotlight on him: "Are you engaged in such a repetition now, with me? Have you left anyone behind?"

"My wife hates this place," said the Doctor simply. "She comes here rarely. She stays in Mexico City most of the time, on the excuse that the children must go to good schools. She is jealous of my patients, and says they are not really ill, that they pretend to be. And in this she is right. Tourists in strange countries are easily frightened. More frightened of strangeness. They call me to reassure themselves that they will not succumb to the poison of strangeness, to unfamiliar foods, exotic flavors, or the bite of an unfamiliar insect. They do call me for trivial reasons, often out of fear. But is fear trivial? And my native patients do need me desperately . . . I built a beautiful house for my wife. But I cannot keep her here. And I love this place, the people. Everything I have created is here. The hospital is my work. And if I leave, the drug traffic will run wild. I have been able to control it."

Lillian no longer resented the Doctor's probings. He was suffering and it was this which made him so aware of others' difficulties.

"That's a very painful conflict, and not easily solved," she said. She wanted to say more, but she was stopped by a messenger boy with bare feet, who had come to fetch the Doctor on an emergency case.

Lillian and the Doctor sat in a hand-carved canoe. The pressure of the human hand on the knife had made uneven indentations in the scooped-out tree trunk which caught the light like the scallops of the sea shell. The sun on the high rims of these declivities and the shadows within their valleys gave the canoe a stippled surface like that of an impressionist painting, made it seem a multitude of spots moving forward on the water in ripples of changeable colors and textures.

The fisherman was paddling it quietly through the varied colors of the lagoon water, colors that ranged from the dark sepia of the red earth bottom to silver gray when the colors of the bushes triumphed over the earth, to gold when the sun conquered them both, to purple in the shadows.

He paddled with one arm. His other had been blown off when he was a young fisherman of seventeen first learning the use of dynamite sticks for fishing.

The canoe had once been painted in laundry blue. This blue had faded and become like the smoky blue of old Mayan murals, a blue which man could not create, only time.

The lagoon trees showed their naked roots, as though on stilts, an intricate maze of silver roots as fluent below as they were interlaced above, and overhung, casting shadows before the bow of the canoe so dense that Lillian could scarcely believe they would open and divide to let them through.

Emerald sprays and fronds projected from a mass of wasp nests, of pendant vines and lianas. Above her head the branches formed metallic green parabolas and enameled pennants, while the canoe and her body accomplished the magical feat of cutting smoothly through the roots and dense tangles.

The boat undulated the aquatic plants and the grasses that bore long plumes, and traveled through reflections of the clouds. The absence of visible earth made Lillian feel as if the forest were afloat, an archipelago of green vapors.

The snowy herons, the shell-pink flamingos meditated upon one leg like yogis of the animal world.

Now and then she saw a single habitation by the waterside, an ephemeral hut of palm leaves wading on frail stilts and a canoe tied to a toy-sized jetty. Before each hut, watching Lillian and the Doctor float by would be a smiling woman and several naked children. They stood against a backdrop of impenetrable foliage, as if the jungle allowed them, along with the butterflies, dragonflies, praying mantises, beetles, and parrots, to occupy only its fringe. The exposed giant roots of the trees made the children seem to be standing between the toes of Gulliver's feet.

Once when the earth showed itself on the right bank, Lillian saw on the mud the tracks of a crocodile that had come to quench his thirst. The scaly carapaces of the iguanas were colored so exactly like the ashen roots and tree trunks that she could not spot them until they moved. When they did not move they lay as still as stones in the sun, as if petrified.

The canoe pushed languid water lettuce out of the

way, and water orchids, magnolias, and giant clover leaves.

A flowing journey, a contradiction to the persistent dream from which Lillian sought to liberate herself. The dream of a boat, sometimes large and sometimes small, but invariably caught in a waterless place, in a street, in the jungle, in the desert. When it was large it was in city streets, and the deck reached to the upper windows of the houses. She was in this boat and aware that it could not float unless it were pushed, so she would get down from it and seek to push it along so that it might move and finally reach water. The effort of pushing the boat along the street was immense and she never accomplished her aim. Whether she pushed it along cobblestones or over asphalt, it moved very little, and no matter how much she strained she always felt she would never reach the sea. When the boat was small the pushing was less difficult; nevertheless she never reached the lake or river or the sea in which it could sail. Once the boat was stuck between rocks, another time on a mud bank.

Today she was fully aware that the dream of pushing the boat through waterless streets was ended. In Golconda she had attained a flowing life, a flowing journey. It was not only the presence of water, but the natives' flowing rhythm: they never became caught in the past, or stagnated while awaiting the future. Like children, they lived completely in the present.

She had read that certain Egyptian rulers had believed that after death they would join a celestial caravan in an eternal journey toward the sun. Scientists had found two solar barques, which they recognized from ancient texts and mortuary paintings, in a subterranean chamber of limestone. The chamber was so well sealed that no air, dust, or cobwebs had been found in it. There were always two such barques—one for the night's journey toward the moon, one for the day's journey toward the sun.

In dreams one perpetuated these journeys in solar

barques. And in dreams, too, there were always two: one buried in limestone and unable to float on the waterless routes of anxiety, the other flowing continuously with life. The static one made the voyage of memories, and the floating one proceeded into endless discoveries.

This canoe, thought Lillian, as she dipped her hand into the lagoon water, was to be her solar barque, magnetized by sun and water, gyrating and flowing, without strain or effort.

The Doctor's thoughts had also b e e n wandering through other places. Mexico City, where his wife was? His three small childen? His past? His medical studies in Paris and in New York? His first book of poems, published when he was twenty years old?

Lillian smiled at him as if saying, you too have taken a secret journey into the past.

Simultaneously they returned to the present.

Lillian said: "There is a quality in this place which does not come altogether from its beauty. What is it? Is it the softness which annihilates all thought and lulls the body for enjoyment? Is it the continuity of music which prevents thoughts from arresting the flow of life? I have seen other trees, other rivers; they did not have the power to intoxicate the senses. Do you feel this? Does everyone feel this? Is this what kept South Seas travelers from ever returning home?"

"It does not affect everyone in the same way," said the Doctor with bitterness in his voice, and Lillian realized he was thinking of his wife.

Was this the mystery in Doctor Hernandez's life? A wife he could not win over to the city he liked, the life he loved?

She waited for him to say more. But he was silent and his face had become placid again.

Her hand, which she had left in the waters of the lagoon to feel the gliding, the uninterrupted gentleness of the flowing, to assure herself of this union with a living current, she now felt she must lift, to prove to the Doctor that she shared his anxiety, and that his sadness affected her. She must surrender the pleasure of touching the flow of water, as if she were touching the flow of life within her, out of sympathy for his anguish.

As she lifted her hand and waited for the drops of water to finish dripping from it, a shot was heard, and water spattered over her. They all three sat still, stunned.

"Hunters?" she asked. She wanted to stand up and shout and wave so the hunters would know they were there.

The Doctor answered quietly: "They were not hunters. It was not a mistake. They intended to shoot me, but they missed."

"But why? Why? You're the most needed, the most loved man here!"

"I refuse to give them drugs. Don't you understand? As a doctor I have access to drugs. They want to force me to give them some. Drugs for forgetting. And I have no right to do this, no right except in cases of great physical pain. That's why when you compared Golconda to a drug I felt bitter. For some people, Golconda is not enough."

The fisherman did not understand their talk in English. He said in Spanish, with a resigned air: "Bad hunters. They missed the crocodile. I could catch him with my bare hands and a knife. I often have. Without guns. What bad hunters!"

The swimming pool was at the lowest level of the hotel and only about ten feet above the sea, so that it was dominated by the roar of the waves hurling themselves against the rocks. The quietness of its surface did not seem like the quietness of a pool but more like that of a miniature bay formed within rocks which miraculously escaped the boiling sea for a few moments. It did not seem an artificial pool dug into cement and fed by water pipes, but rather one of the sea's own moods, one of the sea's moments of response, an intermittent haven.

It was surrounded by heavy, lacquered foliage, and flowers so tenuously held that they fell of their own weight into the pool and floated among the swimmers like children's boats.

It was an island of warm, undangerous water in which one man at least had sought eternal repose by throwing himself out of one of the overhanging hotel windows. Ever since that night the pool had been locked at midnight. Those who knew that the watchman preferred to watch the dancers on the square and that the gate could easily be leaped over, came to sit there in the evenings before going to sleep. The place was barred to any loud frivolity but open for secret assignations after dancing.

It was also Lillian's favorite place before going to sleep. The gentleness of the water, its warmth, was the lulling atmosphere she had missed when she had passed from childhood to womanhood.

She felt an unconfessed need of receiving from some gentle source the reassurance that the world was gentle and warm, and not, as it may have seemed during the day, cold and cruel. This reassurance was never granted to the mature, so that Lillian told no one of the role the pool played in her life today. It was the same role played by another watchman whom she had heard when she was ten years old and living in Mexico while her father built bridges and roads. The town watchman, a figure out of the Middle Ages, walked the streets at night chanting: "All is well, all is calm and peaceful. All is well."

Lillian had always waited for this watchman to pass

26

before going to sleep. No matter how tense she had been during the day, no matter what catastrophes had taken place in school, or in the street, or at home, she knew that this moment would come when the watchman would walk all alone in the darkened streets swinging his lantern and his keys, crying monotonously, "All is well, all is well and calm and peaceful." No sooner had he said this and no sooner had she heard the jangling keys and seen the flash of his lantern on the wall of her room, than she would fall instantly asleep.

Others who came to the pool were of the fraternity who like to break laws, who like to steal their pleasures, who liked the feeling that at any time the hotel watchman might appear at the top of the long stairs; they knew his voice would not carry above the hissing sea, and that as he was too lazy to walk downstairs he would merely turn off the lights as if this were enough to disperse the transgressors. To be forced to swim in the darkness and slip away from the pool in darkness was not, as the watchman believed, a punishment, but an additional pleasure.

In the darkness one became even more aware of the softness of the night, of pulsating life in the muscles, of the pleasure of motion. The silence that ensued was the silence of conspiracy and at this hour everyone dropped his disguises and spoke from some realm of innocence preserved from the corrosion of convention.

The Doctor would come to the pool, leaving his valise at the hotel desk. He talked as if he wanted to forget that everyone needed him, and that he had little time for pleasure or leisure. But Lillian felt that he never rested from diagnosis. It was as if he did not believe anyone free of pain, and could not rest until he had placed his finger on the core of it.

Lillian now sat in one of the white string chairs that looked like flattened harps, and played abstractedly with the white cords as if she were composing a song.

The Doctor watched her and said: "I can't decide which

27

of the two drugs you need: the one for forgetting or the one for remembering."

Lillian abandoned the harp chair and slipped into the pool, floating on her back and seeking immobility.

"Golconda is for forgetting, and that's what I need," she said, laughing.

"Some memories are imbedded in the flesh like splinters," said the Doctor, "and you have to operate to get them out."

She swam underwater, not wanting to hear him, and then came up nearer to where he sat on the steps and said: "Do I really seem to you like someone with a splinter in her flesh?"

"You act like a fugitive."

She did not want to be touched by the word. She plunged into the deep water again as if to wash her body of all memories, to wash herself of the past. She returned gleaming, smooth, but not free. The word had penetrated and caused an uneasiness in her breast like that caused by diminished oxygen. The search for truth was like an explorer's deep-sea diving, or his climb into impossible altitudes. In either case it was a problem of oxygen, whether you went too high or too low. Any world but the familiar neutral one caused such difficulty in breathing. It may have been for this reason that the mystics believed in a different kind of training in breathing for each different realm of experience.

The pressure in her chest compelled her to leave the pool and sit beside the Doctor, who was looking out to sea.

In the lightest voice she could find, and with the hope of discouraging the Doctor's seriousnes, she said: "I was a woman who was so ashamed of a run in my stocking that it would prevent me from dancing all evening. . . ."

"It wasn't the run in your stocking. . . ."

"You mean. . . . other things . . . ashamed . . . just vaguely ashamed. . . ."

28

"If you had not been ashamed of other things you would not have cared about the run in your stocking. . . . "

"I've never been able to describe or understand what I felt. I've lived so long in an impulsive world, desiring without knowing why, destroying without knowing why, losing without knowing why, being defeated, hurting myself and others. . . . All this was painful, like a jungle in which I was constantly lost. A chaos."

"Chaos is a convenient hiding place for fugitives. You are a fugitive from truth."

"Why do you want to force me to remember? The beauty of Golconda is that one does not remember. . . . "

"In Eastern religions there was a belief that human beings gathered the sum total of their experiences on earth, to be examined at the border. And according to the findings of the celestial customs officer one would be directed either to a new realm of experience, or back to re-experience the same drama over and over again. The condemnation to repetition would only cease when one had understood and transcended the old experience."

"So you think I am condemned to repetition? You think that I have not liquidated the past?"

"Yes, unless you know what it is you ran away from . . . "

"I don't believe this, Doctor, I know I can begin anew here."

"So you will plunge back into chaos, and this chaos is like the jungle we saw from the boat. It is also your smoke screen."

"But I do feel new . . . . "

The Doctor's expression at the moment was perplexed, as if he were no longer certain of his diagnosis; or was it that what he had discovered about Lillian was so grave he did not want to alarm her? He very unexpectedly withdrew at the word "new," smiled with indulgence, raised his shoulders as if he had been persuaded by her eloquence, and finally said: "Maybe only the backdrop has changed."

29

Lillian examined the pool, the sea, the plants, but could not see them as backdrops. They were too charged with essences, with penetrating essences like the newest drugs which altered the chemistry of the body. The softness entered the nerves, the beauty surrounded and enveloped the thoughts. It was impossible that in this place the design of her past life should repeat itself, and the same characters reappear, as the Doctor had implied. Did the self which lived below visibility really choose its characters repetitiously and with only superficial variations, intent on reproducing the same basic drama, like a well-trained actor with a limited repertory?

And exactly at the moment when she felt convinced of the deep power of the tropics to alter a character, certain personages appeared who seemed to bear no resemblance to the ones she had left in that other country, personages whom she received with delight because they were gifts from Golconda itself, intended to heal her of other friendships, other loves, and other places.

The hitchhiker Fred was a student from the University of Chicago who had been given a job in the hotel translating letters from prospective guests. Lillian called him "Christmas," because at everything he saw which delighted him—a coppery sunrise or a flamingo bird, a Mexican girl in her white starched dress or a bougainvillaea bush in full bloom—he would exclaim: "It's like Christmas!"

He was tall and blond but undecided in his movements, as if he were not sure yet that his arms and legs belonged to him. He was at that adolescent age when his body hampered him, as though it were a shell he was seeking to outgrow. He was still concerned with the mechanics of living, unable as yet to enjoy it. For him it was still an initiation, an ordeal. He still belonged to the Nordic midnight sun; the tropical sun could not tan him, only freckle him. Sometimes he had the look of a blond angel who had just come from a Black Mass. He smiled innocently although one felt sure

30

that in his dreams he had undressed the angels and the choir boys and made love to them. He had the small smile of Pan. His eyes conveyed only the wide expanse of desert that lay between human beings, and his mouth expressed the tremors he felt when other human beings approached him. The eyes said do not come too near. But his body glowed with warmth. It was his mouth, compressed and controlled, which revealed his timidity.

At everything new he marveled, but with persistent reference to the days of his childhood which had given him a permanent joy. Every day was Christmas day; the turtle eggs served at lunch were a gift from the Mexicans, the opened cocoanut spiked with rum was a new brand of candy.

His only anxiety centered around the problem of returning home. He did not have time enough to hitchhike back; it had taken him a full month to get here. He had no money, so he had decided to work his way back on a cargo ship.

Everyone offered to contribute, to perpetuate his Christmas day. But a week after his arrival he was already inquiring about cargo ships which would take him back home in time to finish college, and back to Shelley, the girl he was engaged to.

But about Shelley there was no hurry, he explained. It was because of Shelley that he had decided to spend the summer hitchhiking. He was engaged and he was afraid. Afraid of the girl. He needed time, time to adventure, time to become a man. Yes, to become a man. (He always showed Shelley's photograph and there was nothing in the tilted-up nose, the smile, and her soft hair to frighten anyone.)

Lillian asked him: "Couldn't Shelley have helped you to become a man?"

He had shrugged his shoulders. "A girl can't help a boy to become a man. I have to feel I am one *before I marry*. And I don't know anything about myself . . . or about women

31

. . . or about love . . . . I thought this trip would help me. But I find I am afraid of all girls It was not only Shelley."

"What is the difference between a girl and a woman?"

"Girls laugh. They laugh at you. That's the one thing I can't bear, to be laughed at."

"They're not laughing at you, Christmas. They're laughing because they wish to hide their own fears, to appear free and light, or they laugh so you won't think they take you too seriously. They may be laughing from pleasure, to encourage you. Think how frightened you would be if they did not laugh, if they looked at you gravely and made you feel that their destiny was in your hands, a matter of life and death. That would frighten you even more, wouldn't it?"

"Yes, much more."

"Do you want me to tell you the truth?"

"Yes, you have a way of saying things which makes me feel you are not laughing at me."

"If . . . you experimented with becoming a man before you married your girl, you might also find that it was *because* you were a boy that she loved you. . . . that she loves you for what you are, not for what you will be later. She might love you less if you changed. . . . "

"What makes you think this?"

"Because if you truly wanted to change, you would not be so impatient to leave. Your mind is fixed on the departure times of cargo ships!"

When he arrived at the pool Lililan could almost see him carrying his two separate and contradictory wishes, one in each hand. But at least while he was intent on juggling them without losing his balance, he no longer felt the pain of not living, of a paralysis before living.

His smile at Lillian was charged with gratitude. Lillian was thinking that the primitives were wiser in having definitely established rituals: at a certain moment, determined by the calendar, a boy becomes a man.

Meanwhile Fred was using all his energy in rituals of

his own: he had to master water skiing, he had to be the champion swimmer and diver, he must initiate the Mexicans into his knowledge of jazz, he had to outdo everyone in going without sleep, in dancing.

Lillian had said: "Fears cannot bear to be laughed at. If you take all your fears, one by one, make a list of them, face them, decide to challenge them, most of them will vanish. Strange women, strange countries, strange foods, strange illnesses."

While Fred dived many times into the pool conscientiously, Diana arrived.

Diana had first come to Mexico at the age of seventeen, when she had won a painting fellowship. But she had stayed, married, and built a house in Golconda. Most of the time she was alone; her husband worked and traveled.

She no longer painted, but collected textiles, paintings, and jewelry. She spent her entire morning getting dressed. She no longer sat before an easel, but before a dressing table, and made an art of dressing in native textiles and jewels.

When she finally descended the staircase into the hotel, she became an animated painting. Everyone's eyes were drawn to her. All the colors of Diego Rivera and Orozco were draped on her body. Sometimes her dress seemed painted with large brushstrokes, sometimes roughly dyed like the costumes of the poor. Other times she wore what looked like fragments of ancient Mayan murals, bold symmetrical designs in charcoal outlines with the colors dissolved by age. Heavy earrings of Aztec warriors, necklaces and bracelets of shell, gold and silver medallions and carved heads and amulets, animals and bones, all these caught the light as she moved.

It was her extreme liveliness that may have prevented her from working upon a painting, and turned a passion for color and textures upon her own body.

Lillian saw her once, later, at a costume party carrying an empty frame around her neck. It was Diana's head

33

substituted for a canvas, her head with its slender neck, its tousled hair, tanned skin and earth-colored eyes. Her appearance within an empty frame was an exact representation of her history.

With the same care she took in dressing herself, in creating tensions of colors and metals, once she had arrived at the top of the staircase she set out to attract all the glances, exposing the delicately chiseled face belonging to a volatile person and incongruously set upon a luxurious body which one associated with all the voluptuous reclining figures of realistic paintings. When she was satisfied that every eye was on her, she was content, and could devote herself to the second phase of her activity.

First of all she thrust her breasts forward, as if to assert that hers was a breathing, generous body, and not just a painting. But they were in curious antiphony, the quick-turning sharp-featured head with its untamed hair, and the body with its separate language, the language of the strip teaser; for, after raising her breasts upward and outward as a swimmer might before diving, she continued to undulate, and although one could not trace the passage of her hand over various places on her body, Lillian had the feeling that, like the strip teaser, she had mysteriously called attention to the roundness of her shoulder, to the indent of her waist. And what added to the illusion of provocation was that, having dressed herself with the lavishness of ancient civilizations, she proceeded gradually to strip herself. It was her artistic interpretation of going native.

She would first of all lay her earrings on the table and rub her ear lobes. The rings hurt her ears, which wanted to be free. No eyes could detach themselves from this spectacle. She would remove her light jacket, and appear in a backless sundress. After breakfast, on a chaise longue on the terrace, she woud lie making plans for the beach, but on this chaise longue she turned in every ripple or motion which could escape immobility. She took off her bracelets and rubbed the wrist which they had confined. She was too warm for her beach robe. By the time she reached the beach even the bathing suit had ceased to be visible to one's eyes. By an act of prestidigitation, even though she was now dressed as was every other woman in the beach, one could see her as the naked, full brown women of Gauguin's Tahitian scenes.

Whoever had voted that she deserved a year to dedicate herself to the art of painting had been wise and clairvoyant.

Illogically, with Diana Fred lost his fear of women who laughed. Perhaps because Diana's laughter was continuous, so that it seemed, like the music of the guitars, an accompaniment to their days in Golconda.

Every day Fred wanted Diana and Lillian to accompany him in his visits to the cargo ships which were to sail him home. The one that had accepted him was not ready yet. It was being loaded very slowly with cocoanuts, and dried fish, with crocodile skins, bananas, and baskets.

They would walk the length of the wharf watching the fishermen catching tropical fish, or watching the giant turtle that had been turned on its back so that it would not escape until it was time to make turtle soup.

Watching the small ships preparing to sail, questioning the captain who wore a brigand's mustache, the mate who wore no shirt, and obtaining no definite sailing date, the anxiety of Christmas reached its culmination.

He had something to prove to himself which he had no yet proved. He was simultaneously enjoying his adventure and constantly planning to put an end to it.

When the captain allowed him to visit the ship he would stand alone on its deck and watch Diana and Lillian standing on the wharf. They waved good-by in mockery and he waved back. And it was only at this moment that he noticed how alive Lillian's hair was, as if each curl were weaving itself around his fingers, how slender Diana's neck and inviting to the hand, how full of light both their faces were, how their fluttering dresses enveloped and caressed them.

Behind them rose the soft violet mountains of Golconda. He had known intimately neither woman nor city and was already losing them. Then he felt pain and a wild desire not to sail away. He would run down the gangplank, pushing the porters to one side, run back once more to all the trepidations they caused him by their nearness.

Neither Diana nor Lillian was helping him. They both smiled so gayly, without a shadow of regret, and did not force him to stay, or cling to him. And in the deepest part of himself he knew they were helping him to become a man by allowing him to make his own decisions. That was part of the initiation. They would not steal his boyhood; he must abdicate it.

He loved them both, Diana for incarnating the spice, the color, and the fragrance of Golconda, and Lillian because her knowledge of him semed to incarnate him, and because she was like a powerful current that transmitted life to him.

Just as he climbed the gang plank as a rehearsal for his departure, he felt then that he was not ready to leave, so when he returned to them he felt unready to live, painfully poised between crystallizations. He could not follow Diana's invitations into the unknown, unfamiliar life of the senses, and he could not sail either.

An invisible race was taking place between Diana's offer of a reclining nude by a Gauguin and the ship's departure. And as if the ship, the captain, the mate, and the men who loaded it had known he was not ready to leave, one day when he went to the pier at four o'clock as he did every day, the ship was gone!

He could still see it on the horizon line, a small black speck throwing off not quite enough smoke to conceal its departure.

36

Lillian was walking through the market. It was like walking through an Oriental bazaar. Gold filigree from Spain, silk scarves from India, embroidered skirts from Japan, glazed potteries from Africa, engraved copper from Morocco, sculptures from Egypt, herbs and incense from Arabia. At the time Golconda was an important seaport, every country had deposited some of its riches there. When it was no longer visited, the Mexicans themselves had created variations upon these themes, adding inventions of their own.

Cages containing tropical birds were panoplied with striped awnings like the tents of ancient maharajahs. From them the Mexicans had inherited the art of training birds to pick out of their hands tiny folded papers containing predictions for the future.

Lillian gave her pennies to the man and asked for one of the messages. The bird very delicately selected, from a handful, a message that read: "You will find what you are seeking." Lillian smiled. She wondered whether among those tiny folded papers the bird might pick up a message telling her *what* it was she was seeking. She decided to squander a few more pennies. But the Mexican bird trainer refused to let her try again. "It's bad luck to question destiny twice. If it gives you two answers you will be confused."

Beside her stood a man who was well known in Golconda as a guide. She had always disliked him. Not because she condemned his trade of selling Golconda to the spectators who could not discover it for themselves, not because she lacked sympathy for the strangers who wanted to witness other's weddings, other's fiestas, as paying guests, but because wherever he stood, at the hotel entrance, at the

37

ticket agencies, at the bullfight entrance, he had the air of a pimp, a pimp who was ashamed of what he was selling, as if Golconda were not a radiant city but a package of obscene post cards. It was the suggestive way he had approached her the first time, whispering: "Would you like to attend a genuine Mexican wedding?" as though he were saying: "would you like me to procure for you a fine young man?"

It may be that Lillian identified his yellow face, his averted eyes, and his constantly nibbling lips with prying, with the spectator, with all peripheral living. And yet, she thought, blushing, I am quite willing to seek guidance for my inward journeys. To ask of a trained bird that he should pick out of a pile of folded papers guidance for my inward journeys!

This thought caused her to look at the guide with more tolerance, and he sensed her weakening defenses. This made him take a step forward and whisper to her shoulder, which was on the level of his eyes: " I have something to show you that will really interest you. It isn't just an ordinary tourist sight, believe me. It is a fellow American in trouble. You're an American woman, aren't you? I was told about you. You came to Mexico as a child with your American father who was an engineer. You speak Spanish fluently, and you understand our ways. I saw you at church with a handkerchief on your head to show respect for our customs. But you are American, I know. Would you feel sorry for an American in real trouble? Would you like to help?"

Lillian struggled with her distrust of the guide, whose lizard-colored eyes remained fixed on the freckles on her shoulders.

"What kind of trouble?"

"Well, he was caught without papers, traveling in the bus to Yucatan. So they put him in jail, here, where he started from. He's been in jail one year now."

"A year? And nothing was done for him?"

38

The guide's mouth, which seemed to nibble and chew at words rather than utter them, nibbled in the void, uttering no word,while he was thinking.

"An American trapped in a foreign country, who cannot speak Spanish. You might at least talk with him?"

"And nothing has been done? Nobody has done anything? Hasn't he appealed to the American consulate?"

The guide mimicked a gesture of indifference, not content with shrugging the imaginary weight off his shoulders, but also washing his hands of it, and when turning away and taking several steps indicating detachment from the problem. It was almost as if he were anticipating any gesture of indifference Lillian might make.

"Where is this jail?"

He walked furtively ahead of her. Whether or not he felt ashamed of taking strangers through the scenes of his native village, ashamed to be paid for invading burials and weddings, he walked as if he were leading them all to places of ill fame, as perhaps he had.

The other tourists treated him with unusual cordiality. They felt isolated and mistook him for a bridge of friendship between themselves and the natives. They fraternized with him as if he were a mediator as well as an interpreter. They drank with him and slapped his back.

But Lillian saw him as the deforming mirror which corrupted every relationship between tourist and native. Only the plight of the American prisoner drove her to follow him through streets she had never crossed before, beyond the market and behind the bullring.

They were in the tenement section, a concentration of shacks built of odds and ends, newspapers on tin slabs, palm trees, driftwood, cartons, gasoline tins. The floors were dirt and hammocks served as beds. The cooking was done out of doors on braziers. No matter how poor the houses, they were camouflaged in flowers, and at each window hung a singing bird. And no matter how poor, the laundry on the

39

line was like a palette from which all the Mexican painters could have drawn their warmest, most burning colors.

Why did the plight of the American prisoner affect her so keenly? The knowledge of his being a stranger in a country whose language he did not speak? She visualized him in jail, drinking the polluted water which made all foreigners sick with dysentery, perhaps being bitten by mosquitoes injecting him with malaria.

All her protectiveness was aroused, so that even the guide no longer seemed like a pimp selling the intimate life of Golconda, but a man of kindness, capable of understanding that tourists could be in genuine trouble and not always absurdly rich and powerful figures.

The jail had been built inside a discarded and ruined church. The ogival windows were heavily barred. The original ochre and coral still remained on the walls and gave the prison a joyous air. The church bells were used to call the prisoners to meals, bedtime, or to announce an escaped convict.

The guide was familiar with the place. The guards did not stop playing cards when he entered. They needed shaves so badly that if they had not worn uniforms one might have taken them for prisoners. The place retained a smell of incense which mixed with the smell of tobacco. Some of the stands which had supported statues now served as coat racks, and gun racks. Belts filled with cartridges were thrown over the holy water stoup. A single statue of the Virgin, the dark-faced one from Guadalupe, had been deemed sufficient to guard the jail.

"*Buenos dias.*"

"*Muy buenos dias.*"

"The lady is here to visit the American prisoner."

One of the guards who had been asleep now pulled out his keys with vague hesitancies. He considered giving the keys to the guide and returning to his siesta, but suddenly his pride awakened and he decided to play his allotted role with exaggerated arrogance.

Inside, the walls of the prison were painted in sky blue. The ceilings retained their murals of nude angels, clouds, and vaporous young women playing harps. The cots were all occupied by sleeping prisoners. The American stood by the iron door of his cell watching the arrival of the visitor.

His thin, long-fingered hands held onto the bars of the cell door as if he would tear them down. But in this lean, unshaved face there was a glint of irony which Lillian interpreted as a show of courage. He was smiling.

"It was good of you to come," he said.

"What can I do for you? Should I telephone the American consulate?"

"Other people have tried that but he will not bother. There are too many of us."

"Too many of you?"

"Well, yes, Americans without papers, runaways from home, runaways from the draft, escaped criminals, displaced persons who claim to be Americans, ex-politicos, ex-gangsters, runaways from wives and alimony. . . ."

"What happened to your papers?"

"I went for a swim one day. I left all my clothes on the beach. When I came back, all my clothes were gone, and with them my papers. So here I am."

He kept his eyes on her face. They were red, probably from not sleeping. The amusement in them might have been a form of courage.

"But what can I do for you? How can I get you out? I'm not rich. I get a small salary for playing the piano at the Black Pearl."

His eyes pleaded softly in contradiction to the clipped words. "The best way to help me is to give the guide fifty dollars. Can you spare that? He will fix things up and get me out. He knows the ropes. Can you manage that?"

"I can do that. But once you're out, how will you get

41

back home, and won't you get caught again without papers?"

"Once I'm out I can hitchhike to Mexico City, and there go to the consulate. I can manage the rest, if you can get me out."

Later on, having delivered the money, she felt immensely light, as if she had freed a part of herself. The prisoner would have haunted her. She knew by the exaggeration of her feelings that there must be some relationship between the condition of the prisoner and herself. What she had felt was more than sympathy for a fellow American. It may have been sympathy for a fellow prisoner.

To all appearances she was free. But free of what? Had she not lost her identity papers? Was not her voyage like that of the South American bird that walked over the sands rubbing out his tracks with a special feather that grew longer than the others, like a feather duster?

The past had been dissolved by the intensity of Golconda, by its light which dazzled the thoughts, closed the eyes of memory. Freedom from the past came with unfamiliar objects; none of them possessed any evocative power. From the moment she opened her eyes she was in a new world. The colors were all hot and brilliant, not the pearly grays and attenuated pastels of her homeland. Breakfast was a tray of fruit of a humid, fleshy quality never tasted before, and even the bread did not have the same flavor. There was an herb which they burned in the oven before inserting the bread which gave it a slight flavor of anise.

All day long there was not a single familiar object to carry her back into her past life. The first human being she saw in the morning was the gardener. She could see him through the half-shut bamboo blinds, raking the pebbles and the sand, not as if he was eager to terminate the task but as if raking pebbles and sand was the most pleasurable occupation and he wanted to prolong his enjoyment. Now and then he would stop to talk with a lonely little girl in a white dress who skipped rope all around him asking questions which he answered gently.

"What makes some butterflies have such beautiful colors on their wings, and others not?"

"The plain ones were born of parents who didn't know how to paint."

And even when familiar objects turned up, they did not turn up in their accustomed places. Like the giant Coca-Cola bottle made of wood placed in the middle of the bull ring before the bullfight began—a grotesque surrealist dream. Lillian had expected the bulls to charge it, but just before the bull was let out the attendants (who usually took care of carrying away the dead bull and sweeping over the bloody tracks) had come and toppled the bottle, and the six of them had carried it away on their shoulders—publicity's defeated trophy.

So all was freedom: her hours, her time, and even the music she improvised at night, the jazz which allowed her to embroider on all her moods.

But there was one moment that was different, and it was the knowledge of this moment that perhaps created her feeling of kinship with the prisoner. That was the hour just before dinner, when she was freshly bathed and dressed, the hour when a genuine adventurer would reach the high point of his gambling with the beauty of the night and feel: Now the evening is beginning and I will discover a human being to court or to be courted by, an adventure with caprice and desire, and while gambling I might find love.

At this hour, when she took one last glance at the mirror, the screen door of her room seemed the locked door of a prison, the room an enclosure, only because she was a prisoner of anxiety: the moment before the unkown gamble with a relationship to other human beings paralyzed her with fear. Who would take her dancing? Would no one come, no one remember her existence? Would all the groups that formed in the evening forget to include her in their plans? Would she arrive at the terrace to find only the head of the Chicago stockyards for a dancing partner? Would she come downstairs and watch Christmas a bemused spectator of Diana's provocations, and couples climbing into cars going to fiestas, and couples climbing the hill to attend the Sunday-night dance on the rocks, and Doctor Hernandez appropriated by a movie star who was sure she had malaria?

This was the moment which proved she was a prisoner of timidities and not a genuine adventurer, not a gambler who could smile when he lost, who could be invulnerable before an empty evening, or untouched by an evening spent with a drunken man who insisted on describing to her how the stockyards functioned, how the animals were killed.

This fantasy of disaster never actually took place. Several people always gathered around the piano when she played and waited for her to stop to offer her a drink and join them. But actual happenings never freed her of her inner imprisonment by fear, in anticipation of aloneness.

She would like to have seen the prisoner again but imagined he was already on his way to Mexico City. She had time to walk down to the Spanish restaurant on the square, which she preferred to the hotel. In the hotel she ate her own dinner in privacy. On the square she felt she had dinner with the entire city of Golconda, and shared a multitude of lives.

The square was the heart of the town. The church opened its doors to it on one side. The other sides were lined with cafés, restaurants with their tables on the sidewalk, a movie house; in the center was a bandstand surrounded by a small park with benches.

On the benches sat enraptured young lovers, tired hobos, men reading their newspapers while little boys shined their shoes. There was also a circle of vendors sitting on the sidewalk with their baskets full of candied fruit, colored fruit drinks, red and yellow cigarettes, and magazines. Old ladies with black shawls walked quietly in and out of the church, children begged, marimba players settled in front of each café and played as long as the pennies flowed. Singers stopped to sing. Little girls sold sea-shell necklaces and earrings. The prostitutes paraded in taffeta dresses with flowers in their black hair.

The flow of beggars was endlessly varied. They changed their handicaps. When they tired of portraying blindness they suddenly appeared with wooden legs. The genuine ones were terrifying, like nightmare figures: a child, shriveled and shrunken, lying on a little table with wheels which he pushed with withered hands; an old woman so twisted she resembled the roots of a very ancient tree; many of them sightless, with festering sores in place of eyes. But they resisted all professional help, as Doctor Hernandez had told her. They refused to be taken out of the streets, from the spectacles of religious processions, Indian fireworks, band concerts, or the flow of visitors in their eccentric costumes.

And among them now, sitting at a nearby table, was the American prisoner with the guide.

From the heightened tones of their voices, the numerous empty bottles of tequila on the table Lililan knew to what cause her donation for freedom had been diverted. They were beyond recognizing her. Unfocused eyes, vague gestures, revealed a Coney Island of the mind, with the whirlings, the crack-the-whips, the dark chambers of surprises, the deforming mirrors, the jet-plane trips, the death-defying motorcycles of drunkenness. Tongues rubberized, their words came out on oiled rollers, their laughter like sudden geysers.

Just as Lillian sat down there came to her table a short Irishman with an ageless face and round, absolutely fixed round eyes. Their roundness and fixity gave his face an expression of extreme innocence. He greeted her and asked her permission to sit down.

He wore white pants as the Mexicans did, a blue shirt open at the neck, and Spanish rope shoes, and talked briefly

45

in such a monotone that it was difficult to hear what he said.

But his pockets were filled with small fragments from excavations, heads, arms, legs, snakes, flutes, pottery of various Indian origins. He would pull one of these objects out of his pocket and hold it for inspection in the palm of his hand. And quietly he would tell the history of the piece.

He never asked anyone to buy them, but if a tourist asked: "Will you sell it?" he assented sadly, as if it belonged to a private collection and he was only a courteous host.

Every time he saw Lillian he showed her one of the pieces and taught her how to distinguish between the periods, by whether the piece was clay or stone, by the slant of the eye, the headgear, the design of the jewels, so that she began to know the history of Mexico.

O'Connor never talked of anything but the new excavations he had attended, the history of the little fragments. And after that he would fall into a tropical trance.

The theatrical scenes on the square sufficed for his happiness—two sailors quarreling, lovers meeting, a Mexican family celebrating their daughter's winning of the Carnival beauty-queen contest, men alone playing chess after dinner. He lived the life of others. Lillian could see him watching these people until he *became* them. He sat in his chair like a body empty of its spirit, and Lillian could sense him living the life of the lovers, the life of the sailors.

She felt he would understand the story of the prisoner and laugh with her at her gullibility. But he did not laugh. His eyes for the first time lost their glassy fixity. They moistened with emotion.

"I wish I had been able to warn you . . . . . I never imagined . . . To think you rescued the one prisoner who did not deserve it! I never told you . . . when I'm not working with excavators and anthropologists I spend all my time rescuing foreigners in trouble—a sailor who gets into a brawl with a Mexican; a tourist whose car kills a donkey on the road. If they are poor, or if they strike a native, the Mexi-

46

cans are apt to forget them in jail. This place is filled with people who don't care what happens to others. They have come here for pleasure. They are running away from burdens. There's something in the climate too. And now you . . . you went and rescued the one prisoner who makes a profession of this, who shares with the guide what the tourists give him, who lives on that, and then quickly returns to jail, to wait for more."

Lillian laughed again, irrepressibly.

"I'm glad you're laughing. I guess I have taken all this too seriously. It has seemed to me almost a matter of life and death, to get all the prisoners out. I never quite understood it. Sometimes I forget them for a few days, go on my expeditions, swim, travel. But always I return to the jail, to the jailed."

"When you're so intent on freeing others you must be trying to free some part of yourself too."

"I never gave it much thought . . . but the desperation with which I work, the amount of time I spend on this, as if it were a vice I had no control over . . . Opening jail doors, and searching for fragments of vanished civilizations. Never thought what it might mean . . . you see, I came here to forget myself. I had the illusion that if I engaged in impersonal activities, I would get rid of myself somewhere. I felt that an interest in the history of Mexico and salvaging prisoners meant I had abdicated my personal life."

"Does it disturb you so much to think that perhaps your apparently impersonal activities actually represent a personal drama in which you yourself are involved? That you are merely re-enacting your intimate drama through others, expressing it through others?"

"Yes, it does disturb me. It makes me feel I have failed to escape from myself. Yet I have known all along that I failed in some way. Because I should have been content, alive, as people are when they give of themselves. Instead I have often felt like a depersonalized ghost, a man without a self, a zombie. It is not a good feeling. It's like the old stories about the man who lost his shadow."

"You never abdicate the self, you merely find new ways of manifesting its activities."

"If you know what they mean, my two obsessions, then tell me, I would rather know. I know I have been deceiving myself. Before we began to talk tonight, when I first sat down with you, I thought myself, "Now I will act like a dead man again, talk like a guide about my new pieces. . . .""

"We never cast off the self. It persists in living through our impersonal activities. When it is in distress it seeks to give messages through our activities."

"Are you trying to say that I was one of the prisoners myself?"

"Yes, I would say that at some time or other you were in bondage, figuratively speaking, at least kept from doing what you wanted to do; your freedom was tampered with."

"Yes, it's true."

"And every time you can get one of those jail doors open, you feel you are settling an account with some past jailer . . . or at least trying to, as I tried today . . . ."

"Very true. At fifteen I had such a passion for archaeology that I ran away from home. I tried to get to Yucatan. The family sent police after me, who caught me and brought me back. From then on they kept me under watch."

Then his look turned once more toward the square, and he relinquished this expedition into his personal life. His eyes became round again and fixed. He had no more to say.

Watching him, Lillian was reminded of the way animals took on the immobility and the color of a tree's bark or a bush so as not to be detected. She smiled at him, but already he was far removed from the present, the personal, as if he had never talked to her, or known her.

She felt that imprisonment had deprived him of communication with his family, that it was his tongue he had lost then, a vital fragment of himself, and that no matter

48

how many statues he unearthed and reconstructed, no matter how many fragments of history he reassembled, one part of him was missing and might never be found.

The marimba players interrupted their playing as if their instruments were a juke box that could not function without the proper amount of nickels, and began to ask for contributions.

In the morning it was the intense radium shafts of the sun on the seas that awakened her, penetrating the native hut. The dawns were like court scenes of Arabian magnificence. The tent of the sky took fire, a laminated coral, dispelling all the sea-shell delicacies which had preceded the birth of the sun, and it was a duel between fire and platinum. The whole sea would seem to have caught fire, until the incendiary dawn stopped burning. After the fire came a rearrangement of more subtle brocades, the turquoise and the coral separated, and transparencies appeared like curtains of the sheerest sari textiles. The rest of the day might have seemed shabby after such an opening, but not in Golconda. The dawn was merely the rain of colors from the sky which the earth and the sea would orchestrate all day, with fruits, flowers, and the dress of the natives. These were not merely spots of color, but always vividly shining and humid, as shining as human eyes, colors as alive as flesh tones.

Just as music was an unbroken chain in Golconda, so were the synchronizations of color. Where the flowers ended their jeweled displays, their pagan illuminated manuscripts, fruits took up the gradations. Once or twice, her mouth full of fruit, she stopped. She had the feeling that she was eating the dawn.

Lying in her hammock she could see both sea and the sunlight, and the rocks below between the stellated, swaying palms. From there too she could see the gardener at work with the tenderness which was the highest quality of the Mexican, a quality which made him work not just for a living, with indifference, but with a tenderness for the plants, a caressingness toward the buds, a swinging rhythm with the rake which made work seem like an act of devotion.

Her day was free until it was time to play with the orchestra for the evening cocktails and dancing.

Before, she had had the feeling that festivities began only with the evening, with the jazz musicians, but now she saw that they began with the sun's extravagance, and ended with a night which never closed up the flowers, or put the gardens to sleep, or made the birds hide their heads in their wings. The night came with such a softness that a new kind of life blossomed. If one touched the sea at night, sparks of phosphorus illuminated it, and sparkled under one's step on the wet sand.

Sometimes, at the beach, the sea seemed not like water but a pool of mercury, so iridescent, so clinging. Swimming on her back, she could see the native musicians arrive, and she would swim ashore.

A guitarist, a violinist, a cellist, and a singer would cluster around an umbrella. The singer sang with such sweetness and tenderness that the hammocks stopped swaying. He enchanted not only the bathers, but the other musicians as well, and the cellist would close his heavy-lidded eyes and play with such a relaxed hand that his brown arm seemed to be held up not by the weight of the hand on the bow, but by some miraculous yogi means of suspension. The South Sea Island shirt seemed to contain no nerves or muscles. The violinist played with one string missing, but as the sea occasionally carried away a few of the notes anyway no one detected the missing ones.

The waves, attracted by the music, would unroll like

a bolt of silk, each time a little closer to the musicians, and aim at surrounding the peg of the cello dug deep into the sand. The cellist did not seem to be looking at the waves, yet each time they moved to encircle his cello, he had already lifted it up in midair and continued to play uninterruptedly while the waves washed his feet, then retreated.

After the musicians came children carrying baskets on their heads, selling fruit and fried fish. Then came the old photographer with his old-fashioned accordion box camera, and a big black box cover for his head. He was so neatly dressed, his mustache so smoothly combed that he himself looked like an old photograph. Someone had touched up the old photographer until he had become a black and white abstraction of old age.

Lillian did not enjoy being photographed, and she sought to escape him by going for a swim. But he was a figures of endless patience, and waited silently, compact, brittle, and straight. The wrinkles of his face all ran upward, controlled by an almost perpetual smile. He was like the old gardener, so ritualistic in his work, so stylized in his dignity, that Lillian felt she owed him an apology: "I'm sorry I kept you waiting."

"No harm done, no harm done," he said gently, as he proceeded to balance his camera on the sand, and just before disappearing under the black cloth he said: "We all have much more time than we have life!"

Watching Lillian being photographed was Edward, the ex-violinist with red hair and freckles who lived in a trailer on the beach. His calendar of events was determined by his multiple marriages. "Oh, the explosion of the yacht? That happened at the time of my second wife." Or if someone tried to recall when the American swimming champion had dived into the rocks: "Oh that was four wives back!" The wives disappeared, but the children remained. They were so deeply tanned it was difficult to distinguish them from the native children. Edward worked at odd jobs: designing

51

fabrics, tending silver shops, or building a house for someone. At the time Lillian met him he was distributing Coca-Cola calendars all over Mexico. To his own amazement, the people loved them and hung them up on their walls. The last one, which he now unrolled to create a stir among the bathers, was an interpretation of a Mayan human sacrifice. The Yucatan pyramid was smaller than the woman, and the woman who was about to be sacrificed looked like Gypsy Rose Lee. The shaved and lean priest looked unequal to the task of annihilating such splendor of the body. The active volcano on the right-hand side was the size of the sacrificial virgin's breast.

Tequila always brought out in Edward a total repudiation of art. He was emphatic about the fact that he had deserted the musical world of his own volition. "In this place music is not necessary. Golconda is full of natural music, dance music, singing music, music for living. The street vendors' tunes are better than any modern composition. Life itself is full of rhythm, people sing while they work. I don't miss concerts or my own violin at all!"

The second glass of tequila unleashed reminiscences of concert halls, and the Museum of Modern Art, as if they had been his residence prior to Golconda. With the third glass came a lecture on the superfluity of art. "For example, here, with the lagoon, the jungle, you do not need the collages of Max Ernst, his artificial lagoons and swamps. With the deserts and sand dunes, the bleaching bones of cows and donkeys, there is no need of Tanguy's desert scenes and bleaching bones. And with the ruins of San Miguel what need do we have of Chirico's columns? I lack nothing here. Only a wife willing to live on bananas and cocoanut milk."

"When I felt cold," said Lillian, "I used to go to the Tropical Birds and Plants Department at Sears Roebuck. It was warm, humid, and pungent. Or I would go to look at the tropical plants in the Botanical Gardens. I was looking for Golconda then. I remember a palm tree there which grew so tall, too tall for the glass dome, and I would watch it pushing against the glass, wishing to grow beyond it and be free. I think of this caged palm tree often while I watch the ones of Golconda sweeping the skies."

But at the third glass of tequila, Edward's talk grew less metallic, and his glance would fall on his left hand where a finger was missing. Everyone knew, but he never mentioned it, that this was the cause of his broken career as a violinist.

Everyone knew too that his children were loved, nourished, and protected by all in Golconda. They had mysteriously accepted an interchangeable mother, one with many faces and speaking many languages, but for the moment it was Lillian they had adopted, as if they had sensed that in her there was a groove for children, already formed, once used, familiar, and which they found comfortable. And Lillian wondered at their insight, wondered how they knew that she had once possessed, and lost, children of the same age.

How did they know she had already kissed such freckles on the nose, such thin elbows, braided such tangled hair, and known where to find missing shoes? It was not only that they allowed her to play the missing mother, but that they seemed intent on filling an empty niche in her, on playing the missing children.

She and the children embraced each other with a knowledge of substitution which added to their friendship, a familiarity the children did not feel with their other temporary mothers.

To her alone they confessed their concern with their father's next choice of a wife. They examined each newcomer gravely, weighing her qualifications. They had observed one infallible sign: "If she loves us first," they explained, "Father doesn't like it. If she loves him first then she doesn't want us around."

An airline's beauty queen arrived at the beach. She walked and carried herself as if she knew she were on display and should hold herself as still as possible, arranged for other's eyes as if to allow them to photograph her. The way she held herself and did not look at others, made her seem an image cut out of a poster which incited young men to go to war. A surface unblurred, unruffled, no frown of thought to mar the brow, she exposed herself to other's eyes with no sign of recognition. She neither transmitted nor received messages to and from the nerves and senses. She walked toward others without emitting any vibrations of warmth or cold. She was a plastic perfection of hair, skin, teeth, body, and form which could not rust, or wrinkle, or cry. It was as if only synthetic elements had been used to create her.

Edward's children were uneasy with this girl, because they imagined their father would be spellbound by the perfect image she presented, the clear blue eyes, the graceful hair, the flawless profile. But soon ¬he made her own choice of companion and it was the ex-Marine who had been pensioned off for exposing himself voluntarily to an experiment with the atom bomb, and had been damaged inside. No one dared to ask, or even to imagine the nature of the injury. He himself was laconic: "I got damaged inside." No injury was apparent. He was tall, strong, and blond, with so rich a coloring he could not take the sun. His blue eyes matched those of the American airline's beauty queen; both were untroubled and designed to be admired. He was reluctant to tell his story, but when he drank he would admit: "I offered myself as a volunter to be stationed as close as possible . . . and I got damaged, that's all."

Neither one had seemed to make any movement toward the other, but as if they had both been moving in the same sphere, at the same altitude, with the same spectator's detachment, they encountered each other and continued to walk together. They did not keep their eyes fastened on each other as the Mexican lovers did.

They both carried cameras, and they methodically photographed everything. But as for themselves, it was as if they had agreed to reveal nothing of themselves by word or gesture.

Edward treated them casually, like walking posters, like one-dimentional cut-outs. But Lillian believed their facade to be a disguise like any other. "They're just not acquainted with their own selves," she said.

"Will you introduce them?" asked Edward ironically.

"But you know that's a dangerous thing to do. They wouldn't recognize each other; they would treat me like a trespasser, and their unrecognized selves like house breakers."

"It is dangerous to confront people with an image of themselves they do not wish to acknowledge."

These words reawakened in her the sense of danger and mystery she felt each time she saw Doctor Hernandez. She remembered his saying: "I get bored with physical illness, which I have fought for fifteen years. As an amateur detective of secret lives I entertain myself."

Another time he had said: "I'm fully aware, of course, that you've thrown me off the scent, by involving me in the secret lives of all your friends in place of your own. But I will tell you one shocking truth. It's not the sun you're basking in, it's my people's passivity and fatalism. They believe the character of man cannot be altered or tampered with, that man is nature, unpredictable, uncontrollable. They believe whatever he is should be accepted along with poverty, illness, death. The concept of effort and change is unknown. You are born poor, good or bad, or a genius, and you live with that just as you live with your relatives."

"Do people ever run amok in Golconda? As they do in Bali, or Africa, or the South Sea Islands?"

"Yes, they do. Because having based all their lives on resignation, acceptance, humility, passivity, when they find themselves in a trap, they do not know how to defeat it; they only know how to grab a revolver or a knife and kill."

"No one searches for reasons, no one prods?"

"Except me. And I will be punished for it. Whoever tampers with this empathy with animals, this osmosis with light, this absence of thought, is always made the victim of people's hatred of awareness."

"You have anesthetics for physical pain. Why not for anxiety, then?"

"Because they do not cure."

There was a masquerade dance on the Mexican general's yacht.

From its decks fireworks exploded into the bay, and the rowboats which took the guests up to the ladder had to sail courageously through a shower of comet tails.

The Mexican general was the only one who was not disguised. He awaited his guests at the top of the ladder, greeted them with an embrace; his circumference was so wide that all Lillian was able to kiss in response to his embrace was one of the medals on his chest.

From behind masks, feathers, paint, spangles, all Lillian could see at first were eyes, sea-eyes, animal-eyes, earth-eyes, eyes of precious stones. Fixed, mobile, fluid, some were easily caught by a stare, others escaped all but a fleeting spark.

Lillian recognized the Doctor only when he spoke. He was costumed as an Aztec warrior, face and body painted, and he was carrying a sharp-pointed lance, and sharp arrows slung across his neck. It was his turn to inflict deep wounds, like those he was weary of healing. That night his appearance forbade all women to rest their heads upon his shoulder and confess their difficulties. Before they crumpled into wailing children, he would challenge the potential mistress.

When Diana arrived with Christmas walking in her shadow, the Doctor said: "When patients suffer from malnutrition of the senses, I send them to Diana."

Diana, her head emerging from the empty picture frame, wearing a violet face mask and her hair covered with sea weed, was dancing with Christmas.

Christmas was dressed quite fittingly, as a man from another planet, but such affirmation of distance did not discourage Diana. She kissed him, and the frame fell around both their shoulders like a life belt to keep them afloat on the unfamiliar sea of the senses, its swell heightened by the jazz and the fireworks.

A couple was leaning over the railing and Lillian could hear the woman say: "Even if you don't mean it, just for tonight, say you love me, I won't ever remind you of it, I will not see you again, but just for tonight say you love me, say you love me."

Would such a guarantee of freedom from responsibility make of any man a lover and a poet? Bring about a lyrical confession? In the green flare of a fireworks fountain, Lillian saw that the man hesitated to create illusion even for one night, and she thought, he should have been disguised as the greatest of all misers!

The woman in quest of illusion disappeared among the dancers.

Everyone was already dancing the intricate patterns of the mambo, which not only set bodies in motion but generated words which would not have been said without such propulsions.

The Doctor was transformed by his disguise; Lillian was astonished to watch him in the role of ruthless lover who would deal only in wounds in the war of love, none of the consolations. He had separated Diana from Christmas with some ironic remarks, and caused another woman to sit alone among the cordage piled in circles on the deck like sleeping anacondas.

It was not only the champagne Lillian drank, it was the softness of the night so palpable that when she opened her mouth she felt as if she had swallowed some of it: it descended into her arteries like a new drug not yet discovered by the alchemists. She swallowed the softness, and then swallowed the showers of light from the fireworks too, and felt illumined by them. It was not only the champagne, but the merry cries of the native boys diving for silver pieces around the yacht, and then climbing on the anchor chain to watch the festivities.

There were many Golcondas—one above the horizon, dark hills wearing necklaces of shivering lights, one reflected on the satin-surfaced bay, one of oil lamps from the native huts, one of candlelights, one of cold neon lights, the neon cross on the church, the neon eyes of the future, without warmth at all—but all of them looked equally beautiful when their reflections fell into the water.

Doctor Hernandez was dancing with a woman who reminded Lillian of Man Ray's painting of a mouth: a giant mouth that took up all of the canvas. The young man the woman had discarded in order to dance with the Doctor seemed disoriented. Lillian noticed his pallor. Drunkenness? Sorrow? Jealousy? Loneliness?

She said to him: "Do you remember in all the Coney Islands of the world a slippery turntable on which we all tried to sit? As it turned more swiftly people could no longer hold onto the highly waxed surface and they slid off."

"The secret is to spit on your hands."

"Then let's both spit on our hands right now," she said, and the manner in which he compressed his mouth made her fear he would be angry. "We both slipped off at the same moment."

His smile was so forced that it came as a grimace. The cries of the diving boys, the narcotic lights, the carnival of fireworks and dancing feet, no longer reached them, and they recognized the similarity of their mood.

"Every now and then, at a party, in the middle of living, I get this feling that I have slipped off," she said, "that I am becalmed, that I have struck a snag . . . I don't know how to put it."

"I have that feeling all the time, not now and then. How would you like to escape altogether? I have a beautiful house in an acient city, only four hours from here. My name is Michael Lomax. I know your name, I have heard you play."

In the jeep she fell asleep. She dreamed of a native guide with a brown naked torso, who stood at the entrance to an Aztec tomb. Holding a machete, he said: "Would you like to visit the tomb?"

She was about to refuse his invitation when she awakened because the jeep was acting like a camel on the rough road. She heard the hissing of the sea.

"How old are you, Michael?"

He laughed at this. "I'm twenty-nine and you're about thirty, so you need not use such a protective tone."

"Adolescence is like cactus," she said. And fell asleep again.

And she began dreaming of a Chirico painting: endless vistas of ruined columns, and ghostly figures either too large, like ancient Greek statues, or too small as they sometimes appeared in dreams.

But she was not dreaming. She was awake and driving at dawn through the cobblestones of an ancient city.

Not a single house complete. The ruins of a once-sumptuous baroque architecture, still buried in the silence it had been in since the volcano had erupted and half buried it in ashes and lava.

The immobility of the people, the absence of wind, gave it a static quality.

The Indians lived behind the scarred walls quietly, like mourners of an ancient splendor. The life of each family took place in an inner patio, and, as they kept the shutters closed on the street side, the city had the deserted aspect of a ghost town.

Rows of columns no longer supporting roofs, churches open to a vaulted sky, a coliseum's empty seats watching in the arena the spectacle of mutilated statues toppled by the victorious lava. A convent without doors, the nun's cells, prisons, secret stairways exposed.

"Here is my house," said Michael. "It was once a convent attached to the church. The church, by the way, is a historic monument, what's left of it."

They crossed the inner patio with its music of fountains, and entered a high-ceilinged white stucco room. Dark wood beams, blood-red curtains, and wrought-iron grilles on the windows gave the dramatic contrasts which are the essence of Spanish life, a conflict between austerity and passion, poetry and discipline. The high walls gave purity and elevation, the rich voluptuous red primitive ardor; dark wood gave the somber nobilities; the iron grilles symbolized the separation from the world which made individuality grow intensely as it did not grow when all barriers of quality and evaluations were removed.

The church bells tolled persistently although there was not ritual to be attended, as if calling day and night to the natives buried by the volcano's eruption years before.

Walking through the muted streets of the place with Michael, Lillian wondered how the Spaniards and the Mayans now lived quietly welded, with no sign of their past warring visible to the outsider. Whatever opposition remained was so subtle and indirect that neither Spaniards nor visitors were aware of it. Michael repeated many times: "The Indians are the most stubborn people."

In the dark, slumbering eyes, white people could never find a flicker of approbation. The Indians expressed no open hostility, merely silence whenever white people approached them, and their glazed obsidian eyes had the power of reflecting without revelation of feelings, as if they had themselves become their black lacquered pottery. White people would explain how they wanted a meal cooked, a house built, a dress made. In the Indian eyes there was a complete lack of adhesion, in their smile a subtle mockery of the freakish ways of all visitors, ancient or modern. The Indians would work for these visitors, but disregard their eccentricity, and disobey them with what appeared to be ignorance or lack of understanding, but which was in reality an enormous passive resistance to change, which enabled them to preserve their way of life against all outside influences.

The Catholic church bells continued to toll, but in the eyes of the Indians this was merely another external form to be adopted and mysteriously, indefinably mocked. On feast days they mixed totem poles and saint's statues, Catholic incense and Indian perfumes, the Catholic wafer and Mayan magic foods. They enjoyed the chanting, the organ and candlelight, the lace and brocades; they played with pictures of the saints and at the same time with Indian bone necklaces.

The silence of the ancient city was so noticeable and palpable that it disturbed Lillian. She did not know at first what caused it. It hung over her head like suspense itself, as menacing as the unfamiliar noises in the jungle she had crossed on the way.

She wondered what attracted Michael to living here among ruins. It was a city rendered into poetry by its recession into the past, as cities are rendered into poetry by the painters because of the elements left out, allowing each spectator to fill in the spaces for himself. The missing elements on the half-empty canvas were important because they were the only spaces in which human imagination could draw its own inferences, its own architecture from its private myths, its streets and personages from a private world.

A city in ruins, as this ancient city was, was more powerful and evocative because it had to be constructed anew by each person, therefore enhanced into illimitable beauty, never destroyed or obscured by the realism of the present, never rendered familiar and forced to expose its flaws.

To gain such altitude it was necessary to learn from the artist how to overlook, leave out, the details which weighed down the imagination and caused crash landings.

Even the prisons, where one knew that scenes of horror had taken place, acquired in the sun, under streams of ivy gently bleached by time, a serenity, a passivity, a transmutation into resignation which included forgiveness of man's crimes against man. In time man will forgive even the utmost cruelty merely because the sacred personal value of each man is lost when the father, the mother, son or daughter, brother or sister, wife of this many have ceased to exist—the ones who gave his life its importance, its irreplaceable quality. Time, powerless to love one man, promptly effaces him. His sorrows, torments, and death recede into impersonal history, or evaporate into these poetic moments which the tourists come to seek, sitting on broken columns, or focusing their cameras on empty ransacked tombs, none of them knowing they are learning among ruins and echoes to devaluate the importance of one man, and to prepare themselves for their own disappearance.

The ancient city gave Lillian a constriction of the heart. She was not given to such journeys into the past. To her it seemed like a city mourning its dead, even though it could not remember those it mourned. She saw it as the ruins of Chirico's paintings and asked Michael: "But why the heavy silence?"

"There's no wind here," said Michael.

It was true. The windlessness gave it the static beauty of a painting.

But there was another reason for the silence, which she discovered only in the afternoon. She was taking a sunbath on the terrace, alone.

The sun was so penetrating that it drugged her. She

fell asleep and had a dream. A large vulture was flying above the terrace, circling over her, and then it swooped downward and she felt its beak on her shoulder. She awakened screaming, sat up, and saw that she had not been dreaming, for a vulture had marked her shoulder and was flying away slowly, heavily.

Wherever vultures settled they killed the singing birds. The absence of singing birds, as well as of the wind, was the cause of that petrified silence.

She began to dislike the ancient city. The volcano began its menacing upward sweep at the edge of the city, and rose so steeply and so high that its tip was hidden in the clouds. "I have been up there," said Michael. "I looked down into its gaping top and saw the earth's inside smoldering."

Michael said on Sunday: "I wish you would spend all your free days here, every week."

That evening he and Lillian, and other guests, were sitting in the patio when suddenly there appeared in the sky what seemed at first like a flying comet, which then burst high in the air into a shower of sparks and detonations.

Lillian thought: "It's the volcano!"

They ran to the outside windows. A crowd of young men, carefully dressed in dark suits and gleaming white shirts, stood talking and laughing. Fireworks illuminated their dark, smooth faces. The marimbas played like a concert of children's pianos, small light notes so gay that they seemed the laughter of the instrument.

The fireworks were built in the shape of tall trees, and designed to go off in tiers, branch by branch. From the tips of the gold and red branches hung planets, flowers, wheels gyrating and then igniting, all propelled into space bursting, splintering, falling as if the sun and the moon and the stars themselves had been pierced open and had spilled their jewels of lights, particles of delight.

63

Some of the flowers spilled their pollen of gold, the planets flew into space, discarding ashes, the skeletons of their bodies. But some of the chariot wheels, gyrating wildly, spurred by each explosion of their gold spokes, wheeled themselves into space and never returned in any form, whether gold showers or ashes.

When the sparkles fell like a rain of gold, the children rushed to place themselves under them, as if the bath of gold would transform their ragged clothes and lives into light.

Beside Lillian, Michael took no pleasure in the spectacle. She saw him watching the students with an expression which had the cold glitter of hunger, not emotion. Almost the cold glitter of the hunter taking aim before killing.

"This is a fiesta for men only, Lillian. The men here love each other openly. See, there, they are holding hands."

Lillian translated this into: He wants it to be thus, this is the way he wants it to be.

"They like to be alone, among men. They enjoy being without women." He looked at her this time with malice, as if to observe the effect of his words on her.

"I lived in Mexico as a child, Michael. The women are kept away from the street, from cafes, they are kept at home. But it does not mean what you believe . . . . "

They watched the young men so neatly dressed, standing in the street with their faces turned toward the fireworks. Then they noticed that across the street from Michael's house, one of the windows was brightly lit, and a very young girl dressed in white stood behind the iron railing. Behind her the room was full of people, and the marimbas were playing.

Then there was a silence. One of the young students moved forward, stood under the young girl's window with his guitar and sang a ballad praising her eyes, smile, and voice.

She answered him in a clear, light voice, accepting the

compliment. The young student praised her again and begged admittance to her home.

She answered him in a clear, light voice, accepting this compliment too, smiled at him, but did not invite him in. This meant that his ballad was not considered artful enough.

This was their yearly poetry tournament, at which only excellence in verse counted. It was the bad poets who were left outside to dance among themselves!

One of the student's ballads finally pleased the girl, and she invited him inside. Her family met him at the door, The other students cheered.

Lillian said: "I'm going out to dance with the bad poets!"

"No," said Michael, "you can't do that!"

"Why not?"

"It isn't done here."

"But I'm American. I don't have to conform to their traditions."

Lillian went out. When she first appeared at the door the students all stared at her in awe. Then they murmured with pleasure: "The American is allowed to dance in the streets."

A bolder one asked her to dance. She glided off with him. The marimbas played with a tinkle of music boxes, the resonances of Tibetan bells, and sometimes like Balinese cymbals. The fireworks lighted up the sky and faces.

Other students pressed around her, waiting for a dance. They offered her a flower to wear in her hair. Tactfully, they made a wall against the students who were drunk, shielding her. She passed from the arms of one student to another. As she passed she could see Michael's face at the window, cold and angry.

The dances grew faster and the change of partners swifter. They sang ballads in her ears.

As the evening wore on she began to tire because of the

cobblestones, and she became a little frightened too, because the students were growing more ardent and more intoxicated. So she began to dance toward the house where Michael stood waiting. They realized she was seeking to escape, and the ones she had not yet danced with pressed forward, pleading with her. But she was out of breath and had lost one heel, so she moved eagerly toward the door. Michael opened it and closed it quickly after her. The students knocked on the door and for a moment she feared they would knock it down.

Then she noticed that Michael was trembling. He looked so pale, drawn, unhappy that Lillian asked him tenderly: "What is it, Michael? What is it, Michael? Did you mind my going out to dance? Did you mind that your fantasy about a world without women was proved not true? Why don't you come with me? We're invited to the Queen's house."

"No, I won't go."

"I don't understand you, Michael. You make it so clear that you want a world without women."

"I don't look upon you as a woman."

"Then why should you mind if I go to a party?"

"I do mind."

She remembered that she had come because he seemed in distress; she had come to help him and not to hurt him.

"I'll stay with you, then."

They sat in the courtyard, alone.

If the city we choose, thought Lillian, represents our inner landscape, then Michael has selected a magnificent tomb, to live among the ruins of his past loves. The beauty of his house, his clothes, his paintings, his books, seem like precious jewels, urns, perfumes, gold ornaments such as were placed in the tombs of Egyptian kings.

"A long time ago," said Michael, "I decided never to fall in love again. I have made of desire an anonymous activity."

66

"But not to feel . . . not to love . ... is like dying within life, Michael."

The burial of emotion caused a kind of death, and it was this cadaver of his feelings he carried within him that gave him, in spite of his elegance, and the fairness of his coloring, a static quality, like that of the ancient city itself.

"Soon the rains will come," he said. "The house will grow cold and damp. The roads will become impassable. I had hoped your engagement at the hotel would last until then."

"Why don't you come back to Golconda then?"

"This place suits my present mood," said Michael. "The gaiety and liveliness of Golconda hurts me, like too much light in your eyes."

"What a strange conversation, Michael, in this patio that reminds me of the illustrations for the Thousand and One Nights—the fountain, the palm tree, the flowers, the mosaic floor, the unbelievable moon, the smell of roses. And here we sit talking like a brother and sister stricken by some mysterious malady. All the dancing and pleasure are taking place next door, nearby, and we are exiled from it . . . and by our own hand."

At night her room looked like a nun's cell, with its whitewashed walls, dark furniture, and the barred windows. She knew she would not stay, that what Michael wanted to share with her was a withdrawal from the world.

In the darkness she heard whisperings. Michael was talking vehemently, and someone was saying: "No, no." Then she heard a chair being pushed. Was it Michael courting one of the young students? Michael who had said lightly: "All I ask, since I can't keep you here, is that in your next incarnation you be born a boy, and then I will love you."

One day in Golconda she saw a bus passing by that bore the name of San Luis, the town near Hatcher's place and she climbed on it.

It was brimming full, not only with people, but with sacks of corn, chickens tied together, turkeys in baskets, church chairs in red velvet, a mail sack, babies in arms.

On the front seat sat the young bullfighter she had seen at the arena the Sunday before. He was very young and very slim. His dark hair was now wild and free, not sleek and severely tied as it was worn by bullfighters. In the arena he had seemed taut, all nerves and electric resilience. In his white pants and slack shirt he looked vulnerable and tender. Lillian had seen him wildly angry at the bull, had seen him challenge the bull recklessly because, during one of the passes, it had torn his pants with its horns, had undressed him in public. This small patch of flesh showing through the turquoise brocaded pants, this human, warm flesh glowing, exposed, had made the scene with the bull more like a sensual scene, a duel between aggressor and victim, and the tension had seemed less that of a symbolic ritual between animal strength and male strength than that of a sexual encounter.

This vulnerable exposure had stirred the women, but injured the bullfighters' dignity, made him a thousand times angrier, wilder, more reckless . . . .

The bus driver was teasing him. He said he was going to visit his parents in San Luis. The bus driver thought he was going to visit Maria. The bullfighter did not want to talk. Next to him sat a very old woman, all in black, asleep with a basket of eggs on her knees. When the bus stopped someone got on carrying candelabras.

"Are they moving the whole church?" asked the man

68

carrying turkeys. But though he was standing, he did not dare sit on one of the red velvet praying chairs. He was bartering with the man who carried chickens. The bag filled with corn undulated with each bump on the road. Finally a very small hole was made in the hemp by so much friction, and a few grains of corn began to fall out. At this the chickens, who were all tied together, began to crane their necks, and to mutiny. The owner of the bag became angry and not finding a way to repair it, sat next to it on the floor with his hand on the hole.

In another seat sat an English woman with a young Mexican girl. The woman was a school teacher. Her English clothes were wearing out; they were mended, patched, but she would not change to Mexican clothes. She wore a colonial hat on her sparse yellow hair. The books she carried were completely yellow and brittle, the corners all chewed, the covers disintegrating.

At each station the bus stopped for the bus driver to deliver letters and messages. In exchange for this he was given a glass of beer. "Tell Josefa her daughter had a son yesterday. She'll writer later. She wants you to come to the baptism."

A man climbed in. His pants were held up with a string. His straw hat looked as if the cows had chewed on the edges until they had reached the unappetizing stains of sweat. His shirt had never been washed. He was selling cactus figs.

At the next stop a priest arrived on his bicycle. He had tied his robe with strings so it would not get caught in the wheels. When he jumped off he forgot to liberate himself, and as he began to run toward the bus he fell on the white dusty road. But nobody laughed. They helped him get his chairs and candelabras out of the bus and placed them on the side of the road. The women then picked them up and balancing them on their heads, followed the priest on his bicycle, in the wave of the dust he raised.

The bus seats were of plain hardwood. The bus jumped like a bronco on the rocky, uneven, half-gutted road. Lillian had difficulty staying in her seat. The bullfighter was gently sleeping, and did not seem like the same young man who had suffered a symbolic rape before thousands of people.

Talking to the conductor in a stream of tinkly words like a marimba was a little girl of seven who resembled Lietta, Edward's oldest daughter. Lillian felt all through her body a dissolution of tenderness for Lietta, who, even though she was so deeply tanned, as dark as a Mexican child, had a transparency and openness Lillian loved. As if children were made of phosphorus, and one saw the light shining in them. The transparent child. Her own little girl at home had had this. And then one day they lose it. How? Why? One day for no perceptible reason, they close their thoughts, veil their feelings, and one can no longer read their faces openly as before. The transparent child. Such a delight to look into open naked feelings and thoughts.

The little girl who talked to the bus driver did not mind that he was not listening. Her eyes were so large that it seemed she must see more than anyone, and reveal more of herself than any child. But her eyes were heavily fringed with eyelashes, and she was watching the road.

Lillian herself must have been transparent once, and how did this heavy wall build up, these prison walls, these silences? Unaware of this great loss, the loss of the transparent child, one becomes an actor, whose profession it is to manipulate his face so that others may have the illusion they are reading his soul. Illusion. How she had loved the bullfighter's fury at the bull, this gentle and tender young man sleeping now, so angry he had almost hurled himself upon its horns.

When did opaqueness set in? Mistrust, fear of judgment. The bus was passing through a tunnel.

Lietta. Lillian could not tell if she was trying to under-

70

stand Lietta, or her own children, or the Lietta she had once been. She remembered watching Lietta's diminutive nose twitching almost imperceptibly when she was afraid, when one of the dazzling women approached her father, for instance. Dream of the transparent child.

The bus was like a bronco. Would they be able to stay on it? In the darkness of the tunnel she lost the image of Lietta in her blue bathing suit and found herself at the same age, herself and other children she had played with, in Mexico, at the time her father was building bridges and roads. The beginning was the whistling by which her mother called her in from playing. She had a powerful whistle. The children could hear it, no matter how far they went. Their playground was a city beneath the city, which had been partly excavated to build a subway like the American subway, and then abandoned. Cities in other centuries, once buried by lava, which ran underneath the houses, gardens, streets. Where it ran under streets there were grilles to catch the rain water but most of the time these grilles only served to bring in a diffuse light. People walked over them without knowing they were walking over another city. The neighborhood children had brought mats, candles, toys, shawls, and lived there a life which because of its secrecy seemed more intense than any above the ground. They had all been forbidden to go there, had been warned of wells, sewers, underground rivers.

The children all stayed together and never ventured father than the lighted passageways. They were fearful of getting lost.

From all the corners of the underground city Lillian could hear her mother calling when it was time to come home. She had never imagined she might disregard her mother's whistle. But one day she was learning from a Mexican playmate how to cut animals and flowers out of paper for a fiesta, and was so surprised by the shapes that appeared that when the whistle came, she decided not to

71

hear it. Her brothers and sisters left. She went on cutting out ships, stars, lanterns, suns, and moons. Then suddenly her candle gave out.

Trailing all her streams of paper with her, she walked toward the opening that gave onto their garden wall, trusting in her memory. But the place was dark. Under her feet the clay was dry and soft. She walked confidently, until she felt the clay growing wet. She did not remember any wet clay in the places where they played. She became frightened. She remembered the stories about wells, rivers, sewers. The knowledge that people were walking about free right above her head, without knowing that she was there, augmented her fear. She had never known the exact meaning of death. But at this moment, she felt that this was death. Right above her her family was sitting down to dinner. She could faintly hear voices. But they could not hear her. Her brothers and sisters were sworn to secrecy and would not tell where she was.

She shouted through one of the grilled openings, but the street was deserted at that moment and no one answered. She took a few more steps into the wet clay and felt that her feet were sinking deeper. She stumbled on a piece of wood. With it she struck at the roof, and continued to call. Some of the dirt was loosened and fell on her. And at this she sat down and wept.

And just as she had begun to feel that she was dying, her mother arrived carrying a candle and followed by her brothers and sisters.

(*When you do not answer the whistle of duty and obedience, you risk death all alone in the forgotten cities of the past. When you engage in the delights of creating pink, blue, white animals and towers, ships and starry stems, you court solitude and catastrophe.*

When you choose to play in a realm far away from the eyes of parents, you court death.)

72

For some, Golconda was the city of pleasure which one should be punished for visiting or for loving. Was this the beginning of the adventurers' superstitions, the secret of their doomed exiles from home?

Her father never smiled. He had so much dark hair, even down along his fingers. He drank and was easily angered, particularly at the natives. The tropics and the love of pleasure were his personal enemies. They interfered with the building of roads and bridges. Roads and bridges were the most important personages in his life.

Lillian's mother did not smile either. Hers was the house of no-smile, from her father because the building of bridges and roads was such a grave matter which the natives would not take seriously, and from her mother because the children were growing up as "savages." All they were learning was to sing, dance, paint their faces, make their own toys as the Mexican children did, adopt stray donkeys and goats, and to smile. The Mexican children smiled in such a way that Lillian felt they were giving all they had, all of themselves, in that one smile. So much was said about "economy" in her house, that there was perhaps also an economy of smiles! Did one have to be sparing of them, give half-smiles, small sidelong smiles, crumbs of smiles? Were the Mexican children living in the present recklessly, without thought of the future, and would these dazzling smiles wear out?

A cyclone carried away one of Lillian's father's bridges. He felt personally offended, as if nature had flaunted his dedication to his work. A flood undermined a road. Another personal affront from the realm of nature. Was it because of this that they returned home? Or because there was shooting in the streets, minor revolutions every now and then?

Once during a school concert at which Lillian was playing the piano, there was a shot in the audience. It was intended for the President but merely put out the lights.

73

While people screamed to get out, Lillian had calmly finished her piece. If she had stayed in Mexico; would she have been so different?

Did everyone live thus in two cities at once, one above the ground, in the sun of Golconda, and one underground? And was everyone now and then metamorphosed into a child again?

There must be someone with whom one can hold a dialogue absolutely faithful to the thoughts that go on in one's head?

At a certain point human beings began to veil themselves. The key word was "transparent." Lietta was transparent. The child talking to the bus driver was transparent. The driver was not listening, but the child was willing to be transparent, exposed.

The bus stopped by a wide river, beyond the village of San Luis. It was waiting for the ferry. The ferry was a flat raft made of logs tied together. Two men pushed it along with long bamboo poles. The ferry was halfway back.

An old woman in black had set up a stand of fruit juices and Coca-Cola. The bullfighter was the first one to leap out.

"Are you going to visit your folks, Miguelito?"

"Yes," he answered sullenly. He did not want to talk.

"What's the matter, Miguelito? Usually you're as quick with your tongue as you are with your sword!"

He too, was traveling through two cities at once. Was he still in the arena, still angry at the bull? Was he concerned about the cost of a new suit?

The raft was approaching. And on the raft was Hatcher's jeep.

When he saw Lillian he smiled. "Were you coming to visit me? I would have come to get you."

"I wanted a ride in the bus."

"I'm going to pick up some bottles of water here and going right back. Where is your bag?"

"I don't have any. I'm only free for the week end. I followed an impulse."

"My wife will be glad to see you. She gets lonely up there."

The bottles of water were loaded on the jeep. Then both jeep and bus rolled onto the raft.

Hatcher had hair on his fingers, like her father. Like her father he was always commanding. The raft became his raft, the men his men, the journey his responsibility. He even wanted to change its course, a course settled hundreds of years ago. His smile too was a quarter-tone smile, as if he had no time to radiate, to expand.

Already she regretted having come. This was not a journey in her solar barque. It was a night journey into the past, and the thread that had pulled her was one of accidental resemblances, familiarity, the past. She had been unable to live for three months a new life, in a new city, without being caught by an umbilical cord and brought back to the figure of her father. Hatcher was an echo from the past.

They were leaving the raft, starting their journey through the jungle. A dust road, with just enough room for the car. The cactus and the banana leaves touched their faces. When they were deep in the forest and seemingly far from all villages, they found a young man waiting for them on the road. He carried a heavy small bag, like a doctor's bag. He wore dark glasses.

"I'm Doctor Palas," he said. "Will you give me a ride?"

When he had settled himself beside Lillian he explained: "I just delivered a child. I'm stationed at Kulacan."

He was carrying a French novel like the one Doctor

Hernandez must have carried at his age. Was he bored and indifferent, or was he already devoted to his poor patients? She wanted to ask. He seemed to divine her question, for he said: "Last night I didn't sleep a wink. A workman came in the middle of the night. He had a wood splinter in his eye. I tried to send him away, I hoped he would get tired of waiting, I just couldn't wake up. But he stayed on my porch, stayed until I had to get up. Even in my sleep I heard the way he called me. They call me the way children call their mother. And I have a year of this to endure!"

Between the trees, now and then, there appeared the figure of a workman with a machete. White pants, naked torso, sandals, and a straw hat, bending over their cutting. When they heard the car they straightened up and watched them with somber eyes.

Once one of them signaled Hatcher to stop. Lillian saw him grow tense. Then they pushed before them a frightened child.

"Will you take him? He's too small to walk all the way."

"Climb over the bottles," said Hatcher.

But the child was too frightened. He clung to the extra tire in the back, and when the jeep slowed down before a deep ravine, he leaped off and disappeared into the forest.

"Here is my place," said Hatcher, and turned left up a hill until he reached a plateau. On this open space he had built a roof on posts, with only one wall in the back. The cooking was done out of doors. A Mexican woman was bending over her washing. She only came when Hatcher called her. She was small and heavy, and sad-faced, but she gave Hatcher a caressing look and a brilliant warm smile. Toward the visitors she showed only a conscious effort at politeness.

"You must excuse us, the place is not finished yet. My husband works alone, and has a lot to do."

"Bring the coffee, Maria," said Hatcher. She left them sitting around a table on the terrace, staring at an unbelievable stretch of white sand, dazzling white foam spraying a gigantic, sprawling vegetation which grew to the very edge of the sand. Birds sang deliriously, and monkeys gave humorous clown cries in the trees. The colors all seemed purer, and the whole place as if uninhabited by man.

Maria came with coffee in a thermos. Hatcher patted her shoulder and looked gratefully at her.

"She is the most marvelous wife," he said.

"And he is a wonderful husband," said Maria. "Mexican husbands never go around telling everyone they are married. Whenever Harry goes to Golconda, he keps telling everyone about his wife."

And then, turning to Lillian, she added in a lower tone, while Hatcher talked with the young doctor: "I don't know why he loves me. I am so short and squatty. He was once married to someone like you. She was tall, and she had long, pointed, painted nails. He never talks about her. I worked for him, at first. I was his secretary. We are going to build a beautiful place here. This is only the beginning."

Against the wall at the back they had their bedroom. Lillian could imagine them together. She was sure that he lay with his head on his wife's breast. She was compliant, passive, devoted.

Lillian wondered if he were truly happy. He seemed so intent on affirming his happiness. He was not tranquil, or capable of contemplation. He named all the beauties of his place, summoned them. When he mentioned America, his mouth grew bitter. He missed nothing. American women . . . He stopped himself, as if aware for the first time that Lillian was one of them. His eyes alighted on Lillian's nails. "I hate painted nails," he said. Until now he had been friendly. Something, a shadow of a resemblance, a recall, had sent him for a moment into the city beneath the city, the subterranean chambers of memory. But he leaped back into the present to describe all the work that had yet to be done.

"As you can see, it is still very primitive."

On the terrace, several camp beds were set side by side, as in an army barracks, with screens between them.

"I hope you won't mind sleeping out of doors."

The Mexican doctor was leaving. "Tomorrow I will be driving back with friends who are spending a few days in Golconda. If you want us to, we will pick you up."

Lillian wanted to walk to the beach. She left the Hatchers discussing dinner, and followed a trail down the hill. The flowers which opened their violet red velvety faces toward her were so eloquent, they seemed about to speak. The sand did not seem like sand, but like vaporized glass, which reflected lights. The spray and the foam from the waves was of a whiteness impossible to match. The sea folded its layers around her, touched her legs, her hips, her breasts—a liquid sculptor, the warm hands of the sea all over her body.

She closed her eyes.

When she came out and put on her clothes she felt re-born, born anew. She had closed the eyes of memory. She felt as though she were one of the red flowers, that she would speak only with the texture of her skin, the tendrils of hair at the core, remain open, feel no contractions ever again.

She thought of the simplified life. Of cooking over a wood fire, of swimming every day, of sleeping out of doors in a cot without sheeets, with only a Mexican wool blanket. Of sandals, and freedom of the body in light dresses, hair washed by the sea and curled by the air. Un-painted nails.

When she arrived Maria had set the table. The lights were weak bulbs hanging from a string. The generator was working and could be heard. But the trees were full of fireflies, crickets and pungent odors.

"If you want to wash the salt off, there is a creek just down toward the left, and a natural pool. Take a candle."

"No, I like the salt on my skin."

On the table were dishes of black beans, rice, and tamales. And again coffee in the thermos bottle.

After dinner Hatcher wanted to show Lillian all of the half-built house. She saw their bedroom, with its whitewashed walls and flowered curtains. And behind the wall a vast storage room.

"He is very proud of his storage room," said Maria.

It was enormous, as large as the entire front of the house. As large as a supermarket. With shelves reaching to the ceiling. Organized, alphabetized, catalogued.

Every brand of canned food, every brand of medicine, every brand of clothing, glasses, work gloves, tools, magazines, books, hunting guns, fishing equipment.

"Will you have cling peaches? Asparagus? Quinine?" He was swollen with pride. "Magazines? Newspapers?"

Lillian saw a pair of crutches on a hook at the side of the shelf. His eyes followed her glance, and he said without embarrassment: "That's in case I should break a leg."

Lillian did not know why the place depressed her. She suddenly felt deeply tired. Maria seemed grateful to be left alone with her husband. They went into their bedroom in the back, and Lillian sat on her cot at the front of the open terrace, and undressed behind a screen.

She had imagined Hatcher free. That was what had depressed her. She had been admiring him for several weeks as a figure who had attained independence, who could live like a native, a simplified existence with few needs. He was not even free of his past, of his other wife. The goodness of this one, her warmth, her servitude, only served to underline the contrast between her and the *other*. Lillian had felt him making comparisons between her and his Mexican wife. The *other* still existed in his thoughts. It may even have been why he invited Lillian the very first day in the taxi.

She couldn't sleep, having witnessed Hatcher's umbilical ties with his native land's protectiveness. (America alone could supply crutches if one broke one's leg, America alone could cure him of malaria, America-the-mother, America the-father had been transported into the supplies shed, canned and bottled.) He had been unable to live here naked, without possessions, without provisions, with his Mexican mother and the fresh fruits and vegetables in abundance, the goat's milk, and hunting.

Close the eyes of memory . . . but was she free? Hatcher's umbilical cord had stirred her own roots. His fears had lighted up these intersections of memory which were like double exposures. Like the failed photograph of the Mayan temple, in which by an accident, a failure to turn a small key, Lillian had been photographed both standing up and lying down, and her head had seemed to lie inside the jaws of a giant king snake of stone, and the stairs of the pyramid to have been built across her body as if she had been her own ghostly figure transcending the stone.

The farther she traveled into unknown places, unfamiliar places, the more precisely she could find within herself a map showing only the cities of the interior.

This place resembled none other, with its colonnade of palm-tree trunks, its walled back set against the rocks, its corrugated roof on which monkeys clowned. The cactus at night took shapes of arthritic old men, bearded scarecrows of the tropics, and the palms were always swaying with a rhythm of fans in the heat, of hammocks in the shade.

Was there no open road, simple, clear, unique? Would all her roads traverse several worlds simultaneously, bordered by the fleeting shadows of other roads, other mountains? She could not pass by a little village in the present without passing as well by some other little village in some other country, even the village of a country she had wished to visit once and had not reached!

Lillian could see the double exposure created by memory. A lake once seen in Italy flowed into the lagoon which encircled Golconda, a hotel on a snowy mountain in Switzerland was tied to Hatcher's unfinished mountain home by a long continuous cable, and this folding cot behind a Mexican screen lay alongside a hundred other beds in a hundred other rooms, New York, Paris, Florence, San Francisco, New Orleans, Bombay, Tangiers, San Luis.

The map of Mexico lay open on her knees, but she could not find the thick single line which indicated her journeys. They divided into two, four, six, eight skeins.

She was speeding at the same rhythm along several dusty roads, as a child with parents, as a wife driving her husband, as a mother taking her children to school, as a pianist touring the world, and all these roads intersected noiselessly and without damage.

Swinging between the drug of forgetfulness and the drug of awareness, she closed her eyes, she closed the eyes of memory.

When she awakened she saw first of all a casuarina tree with orange flowers that seemed like tongues of flames. Between its branches rose a thin wisp of smoke from Maria's *brasero*. Maria was patting tortillas between her hands with an even rhythm and at the same time watching over genuine American pancakes saying: "Senorita, I have tortillas *a la Americana* for you."

The table was set in the sun, with Woolworth dishes and oilcloth and paper napkins.

The young doctor had arrived with his friends. They would take her back to Golconda.

Maria was gazing at Lillian pensively. She was trying to imagine that a woman just like this one had hurt

Hatcher so deeply that he never talked about it. She was trying to imagine the nature of the hurt. She knew that Hatcher no longer loved that woman. But she knew also that he still hated her, and that she was still present in his thoughts.

Lillian wanted to talk to her, help her exorcise the American woman with the painted nails. But Hatcher would be lonely without his memories, lonely without his canned asparagus, and his American-made crutches. Did he truly love Maria, with her oily black hair, her maternal body, her compassionate eyes, or did he love her for not being his first wife?

He looked at Lillian with hardness. Because she did not want to stay? Could she explain that she had spent the night in the subterranean cities of memory, instead of outside in the spicy, lulling tropical night?

Doctor Palas had been called during the night, and was in a bad humor. His friends had found the new beach hotel lacking in comfort. "The cot had a large stain, as if a crime had been committed there. The mosquito netting had a hole, and we were bitten by mosquitoes. And in the morning we had to wash our faces from a pail of water. We gave some pennies to the children. They were so eager that they scratched our hands. And only fish and black beans to eat, even for breakfast."

"Some day," said Hatcher, "when my place is built it will attract everyone. I am sure the movie colony will come."

"But I thought you came here to be isolated, to enjoy a primitive life, a simple life."

"It isn't the first time a human being has had two wishes, diametrically opposed," said Doctor Palas.

In the car, driving back in the violent sun, no one talked. The light filled the eyes, the mind, the nerves, the bones, and it was only when they drove through shade that they came out of this anasthesia of sunlight. In the shade they would find women washing clothes in the river,

82

children swimming naked, old men sitting on fences, and the younger men behind the plough, or driving huge wheeled carts pulled by white Brahma bulls. In the eyes of the Mexicans there were no questions, no probings; only resignation, passivity, endurance, patience. Except when one of them ran amok.

Lillian could feel as they did at times. There were states of being which resembled the time before the beginning of the world, unformed, undesigned, unseparated. Chaos. Mountains, sea and earth undifferentiated, nebulous, intertwined. States of mind and feeling which would never appear under any spiritual X-ray. Dense, invisible, inaccessible to articulate people. She would live here, would be lost. At every moment of anxiety, of probing, she would slip into the sea for rebirth. Her body would be restored to her. She would feel her face as a face, fleshy, sunburned, warm, and not as a mask concealing a flow of thoughts. She would be given back her neck as a firm, living, palpitating, warm neck, not as a support for a head heavy with fever and questions. Her whole body would be restored to her, breasts relaxed, no longer compressed by the emotions of the chest, legs restored, smooth and gleaming. All of it cool, smooth, washed of thought.

She would plunge back with these people into silence, into meditation and contemplation. When she washed her clothes in the river she would feel only the flow of the water, the sun on her back. The light of the sun would fill every corner of her mind and create refractions of light and color and send messages to her senses which would dissolve into humid shining fields, purple mountains, and the rhythms of the sea and the Mexican songs.

No thoughts like the fingers of a surgeon, feeling here and there, where is the pain, where did destruction spring from, what cell has broken, where is the broken mirror that distorts the images of human life?

Chaos was rich, destructive, and protective, like the

83

dense jungle they had traveled through. Could she return to the twilight marshes of a purely natural, inarticulate, impulsive world, feel safe there from inquiry and exposure?

But in this jungle, a pair of eyes, not her own, had followed and found her. Her mother's eyes. She had first seen the world through her mother's eyes, and seen herself through her mother's eyes. Children were like kittens, at first they did not have vision, they did not see themselves except reflected in the eyes of the parents. Lillian seen through her mother's eyes.

Her mother was a great lady. She wore immaculate dresses, was always pulling on her gloves. She had tidy hair which the wind could not disarrange, she wore veils, perfume. Lillian's outbursts of affection were always curtailed, because they threatened this organization. "Don't wrinkle my dress. You will tear my veil. Don't muss my hair." And once when Lillian had buried her face in the folds of her dress and cried: "Oh, Mother, you smell so good," she had even said: "Don't behave like a savage." If this is a woman, thought Lillian, I do not want to be one. Lillian was impetuous, but this barrier had driven her into an excess, into exaggerations of her tumultuousness.

She threw her clothes about, she soiled and crumpled up her dresses. Her hair was never tidy. At the same time, she felt that this was the cause of her mother's coolness. She did not want this coldness. She thought she would rather be chaotic, and stutter and be rough but warm. When she disobeyed, when she ran amok, she felt she was rescuing her warmth and naturalness from her mother's formal hands. And at the same time she felt despair, that because she was as she was, and unable to be like HER, she would never be loved. She took to music passionately, and there too her wildness, her lack of discipline, hampered her playing. In music too there was a higher organization of experience. Yes, she knew that, she was undisciplined and wayward. Only today, traveling through Mexico, a country

84

of warmth, of naturalness, and looking into eyes that did not criticize, did she realize she had never yet used her own eyes to look at herself.

Her mother, a very tall woman with critical eyes. She had eyes like Lillian's a vivid electric blue. Lillian looked into them for everything. They were her mirror. She thought she could read them clearly, and what she saw made her uneasy. There were never any words. Only her eyes. Was this dissatisfaction due to other causes? She used her eyes to stop Lillian, when Lillian wanted to draw physically close to her. It was a kind of signal. Her mother had told her only much later, that she did think her an awkward and ardent child, chaotic, impulsive, did think how emotional she was, how she could not civilize her. Those were her mother's words.

Lillian had never seen herself with her own eyes. Children do not possess eyes of their own. You retained as upon a delicate retina, your mother's image of you, as the first and the only authentic one, her judgment of your acts.

They had reached a place of shade by the river. They had to wait for the barge to take them across. They got out of the car and sat on the grass. A woman was hanging her laundry on the branches of a low tree, and the blues, oranges, pinks looked like giant flowers wilted by tropical rains.

Another woman approached them with a basket on her head. She took it down with calm, deliberate gestures and put before them a neatly arranged pile of small fried fish.

"Do you have any beer?" asked Doctor Palas.

The houses by the river did not have any walls. They were palm leaves on four palm trunks. A woman was pushing a small hammock monotonously to keep a baby asleep. Children were playing naked in the dust and by the edge of the river.

It was Doctor Palas' friends who noticed that the radiator was leaking profusely. They would never reach Golconda. They would be lucky if they reached San Luis, on the other side of the river.

Lillian was thinking that at this time Diana, Christmas, and her other friends were starting on a colorful safari to the beach.

The barge drifted in slowly, languidly. The men who had pushed it wiped the perspiration from their shoulders. In their dark red-brown eyes, fawn eyes, there were always specks of gold. From the sun, or from some deep Indian irony. Catastrophe always made them laugh. Was it a religion unknown to Lillian? A dog half drowned once, at the beach, made them laugh. The leaking radiator, the stranded tourists. And this was New Year's Eve. They would not reach Golconda for the fireworks and street dances.

San Luis was a village of dirt streets, shacks, in which bands of pigs were left to find their nourishment in the garbage, and bands of children followed the foreigners asking for pennies. There was only a square, with a church of gold and blue mosaics, a cafe, a grocery, a garage. They took the car there and Doctor Palas translated for them. Lillian understood the palaver. It consisted, on the Indian side, in avoiding a direct answer to a simple question: "When will the car be ready?" As if a direct answer would bring down on them some fatal wrath, some superstitious punishment. It was impossible to say. Would they care to sit at the cafe while they waited? It was four o'clock. They sat there until six. Doctor Palas went back to the garage several times. In between he sought to continue with Lillian an intimate conversation in Spanish which his American friends would not understand. Without knowing the trend of meditation that Lillian had embarked on, on the theme of eyes, the eyes of her mother with which she had looked at herself, it was her eyes he praised, and her hair. Her eyes which were not her own when she looked at herself. But when she looked at others, she saw them with love, with compassion. She truly saw them. She saw the American

86

couple, uncomfortable, not understanding this mixture of dirt and gaiety. The children took delight in chasing away the pigs and imitating their cries.

She saw young Doctor Palas not yet humanly connected with the poor as Doctor Hernandez was.

"Will you go dancing with me tonight?"

"If we get to Golconda," said Lillian, laughing. "I hope the Hungarian violinist will sweep them off their feet, so they will not notice my absence."

At seven o'clock the streets were silent and it began to grow dark. The owner of the cafe was a fair-faced Spaniard, with the manners of a courtier. He was helping them to pass the time. He had sent for a guitar player and a singer. He had fixed them a dinner.

When all of them realized they would not be leaving that night, that the car seemed to be losing vigor rather than regaining it, he came and talked to them with vehemence.

"San Luis looks quiet now, but it is only because they are dressing for New Year's Eve. Pretty soon they will all be out in the streets. There will be dancing. But the men will drink heavily. I advise you not to mix with them. The women know when to leave. Gradually they disappear with the children. The men continue drinking, and soon they begin to shoot at mirrors, at glasses, at bottles, at anything. Sometimes they shoot at each other. I entreat you, *Senores y Senoras* to stay right here. I have clean rooms I can let you have for the night. Stay in our rooms. I strongly advise you . . ."

The rooms he showed them gave on a peaceful patio full of flowers and fountains. Lillian was tempted to go out with the Doctor, at least to dance a while. But traditional protectiveness toward women made him obstinately refuse to take the risk. At ten o'clock the fireworks, the music, and the shouts and quarrels began. They went to their rooms. Lillian's room was like a white nun's cell.

Whitewashed walls, a cot buried in white mosquito netting, no sheets or blankets. The walls did not reach to the ceiling, to let the air through, and her shutter door let in all the sounds of the village. After the fireworks, the shooting began. The cafe owner had been wise.

It was in such rooms that Lillian always made the devastating discovery that she was not free. Out in the sun, with others, swimming or dancing, she was free. But alone, she was still in that underground city of her childhood. Even though she knew the magic formula: life is dreamed, life is a nightmare, you can awaken, and when you awaken you know the monsters were self-created.

If she could have danced with Doctor Palas, maintained the speed of elation, sat at a table and let him rest his hand lightly on her bare arm, participated in a carnival of affection.

All of them with navigation troubles. The American couple fearful of unfamiliarity. Doctor Palas lonely.

I can see, I can see that it is in this distorted vision of the world's proper proportions that lies the secret of our fears. We make the animals bigger with our fears. We make our creations and our loves smaller, we shrink by our vision, and enlarge and shrink according to the whims of our interchangeable vision, not according to an immutable law of growth. The size of each world we live in is individual and relative, and the objects and people vary in each EYE.

Lillian remembered when she had believed that her mother was the tallest woman on earth, and her father the heaviest man. She remembered that her mother never had a wrinkle on her dress, or a lock of hair out of place, and was always putting on her gloves as if she were a noted surgeon about to operate. Her presence was antiseptic, particularly in Mexico, where she was unsuited to the humanity of the life, the acceptance of flaws, spots, stains, wrinkles. Children changed the size of all they saw, but so did the parents, and they continued to see one *small*.

88

She was too cold to fall asleep. The wind from the mountain had descended upon San Luis as soon as the sun had set.

I see my parents smaller, they have assumed a natural size. My father must have been like Hatcher, terribly afraid of a strange country on which he was dependent for a living. But how could my mother's whistle have penetrated through all those underground passages? There must have been an echo!

If she still could hear this whistle, there must be echos in the soul. But she was regaining her own eyes, and with these eyes, with her own vision, she would return home.

The patio was full of birds in cages. The noises of the fiesta kept them awake too. Why should it be among these shadows, these furtive illuminations, these descending passageways that her true self would hide? Driven so far below the surface! She was now like those French speleologists who had descended thousands of feet into the earth and found ancient caves covered with paintings and carvings. But Lillian carried no searchlight, and no nourishment. Nothing but the wafer granted to those who believe in symbolism, a wafer in place of bread. And all she had to follow were the inscriptions of her dreams, half-effaced hieroglyphs on half-broken statues. And no guiding in the darkness but a scream through the eyes of a statue.

In the morning she returned to life above the ground. Outside in the patio there was a washstand, and the water in the pitcher was cool spring water. The mirror was broken, and the towel had been used by many people. But after the loneliness of the night's journey Lillian was happy to use a collective towel and to see her face in two pieces which could be made to fit together again. She had made a long journey, the journey of the smile and the eyes. There were no decorations for such discoveries. The journey had in reality taken only three months. According to the calendar her trip had taken only the time of an engagement in a night club. The

89

voyage underground had taken longer, and had taken her farther. She would return to Golconda to drink her last cup of flowing gold, iridescent water, sun and air, to pack her treasures, her geological discoveries, the statues which, once unearthed, had become so eloquent.

When they arrived at Golconda it was the end of the New Year celebrations. The streets were still littered with confetti. The street vendor's baskets were empty, and they were sleeping beside them rolled in their ponchos. The scent of malabar was in the air, and that of burnt fireworks.

Lillian walked down the hill to the center of town, past the old woman in black who sold colored fruit juices and white cocoanut candy, past the church with its wide doors open so that she could see the bouquets of candlelights and the women praying while they fanned their faces. Cats and dogs were allowed to stray in and out, the workmen continued to work on their scaffolds while Mass was being said, the children were allowed to cry, or were fed right there while lying in the black shawls slung from their mother's necks like hammocks.

She walked in a glittering sunlight that annihilated all thought, that left only the eyes awake, and a procession of images marching through the retina, no thoughts around them, no thoughts interpreting them.

She walked more heavily on her heels, on flat sandals, as the natives walked, and although she weighed exactly the same as when she had first arrived, a medium weight, she felt heavier, and more aware of her body. The swimming, the sun, the air, all contributed to sculpture a firm, elastic, balanced body, free in its movements.

She was preparing herself to talk to the Doctor, as he had wanted her to talk. She had awakened with a clear image of the Doctor's character.

Doctor Hernandez in the taxi, the first day, concerned over his village's state of health, aware of others' moods and needs, unable to forget the secret sorrow of his own life.

90

Doctor Hernandez probing into her life with a doctor's conviction of his right to probe, and evading her questions.

She had seen him in his home, in a Spanish setting, and met his wife, who had come for one of her brief visits. Under a semblance of Latin submission, under her thoughtfulness in serving him his drink, saving him from telephone calls, there was a mockery in his wife's attitude toward his patients. This had been instilled in the children who played the game of "being a doctor" differently from other children; they expressed distaste for his profession. The sick were not really sick, and the sick who came from the poor, with the desperate illnesses that attacked the undernourished natives, both children and wife totally ignored.

Lillian had seen in the Doctor's eyes a sadness which seemed out of proportion to the children's irony. He watched them perform their doctor act. The patient was a beautiful movie star. She was covered with bandages. Doctor Hernandez' daughter took this role. As soon as the "doctor" came near to her, she herself unwound all the bandages, threw herself upon him, embraced him and said: "Now that you have come I am not sick any more."

This morning as she walked, all these fragments had coalesced into the figure of a man in trouble, and Lillian understood that his persistence in making her confess was a defense against all that he himself wanted to confess.

At first she had not understood the game, nor his need. But she did now. And even if it meant that first of all (to play it as he wished it) she must confide in him, she was now willing, because it would liberate him of his secret. It was a habitual role for him to take: that of confessor. In any other role he would be uncomfortable.

The street climbed halfway up the hill, and there was the Doctor's office. The waiting room was a patio, with wicker chairs placed between potted palms and rubber plants. Pink and purple bougainvillaea trailed down the walls. A servant in bedroom slippers was mopping the mosaic floor. The nurse was not dressed like a nurse but, like all the native girls who worked in Golconda, she wore a party dress, a rose pastel taffeta which made her seem much more like a nurse to pleasure than to illness. There were ribbons in her hair, and sea-shell earrings on her ears.

"The Doctor has not yet arrived," she said.

This was no unusual occurrence in the Doctor's life. Added to the demands of his profession and their uncertain timing, was the natives' own religion of timelessness. They absolutely refused to live in obedience to clocks, and it was always their mood that dictated their movements.

But Lillian felt an uneasiness which compelled her to walk instead of waiting patiently in the office.

She walked along the docks, watching the fishermen returning from their day's work. Each boat that had made a large catch had a pennant waving on its mast. The wind caught the banners and imprinted on them the same ripples and billows as it did on the skirts of the women, and the ribbons on their hair.

She sat down at a little cafe and had a dark coffee, watching the boats heaving up and down, and the families taking a walk with all their children. How they installed themselves in the present! They looked at everything that was happening as if nothing else existed, as if there were no work to be done, no home to return to. They abandoned themselves to the rhythm, let the wind animate scarves and hair, as if every undulation and ripple of color and motion hypnotized them into contentment.

By the time she returned to the Doctor's office it was growing dark.

None of the patients showed uneasiness. But the nurse said: "I don't understand. I called the Doctor's home. He left there an hour ago saying he was coming straight to his office."

Just as she turned on the electric lights, they went out again. This often happened in Golconda. The power was weak. But it increased Lillian's anxiety, and to relieve it she decided to walk toward the Doctor's home, hoping to meet him on the way.

The long walk uphill oppressed her. The electric lights were on again, but the houses grew farther apart from each other, the gardens darker and denser as she walked.

Then in an isolated field she noticed a car which had run into an electric pole. A group of people were gathered around it.

In the dark she could not see the color of the car. But she heard the screams of the Doctor's wife.

Lillian began to tremble. *He had tried to prepare her for this.*

She continued to walk. She was not aware that she was weeping. The Doctor's wife broke away from the group and ran toward Lillian, blindly. Lillian took her in her arms and held her, but the woman fought against her. Her mouth was contorted but no sounds came from it, as if her cries had been strangled. The wife fell on her knees and hid her face in Lillian's dress.

Lillian could not believe in the Doctor's death. She consoled the wife as if she were a child with an exaggerated sorrow. She heard the ambulance come, the one he had raised the funds to buy. She saw the doctors, and the people around the car. She realized that it was his car's hitting the pole that had cut off the electric current for a moment. The wife now talked incoherently: "They shot him, they finally shot him . . . they shot him and the car went against the pole. I wanted to get him away from here. Who would be capable of killing such a man? Who? Tell me. Tell me."

Who would be capable of killing such a man? Who, thinking of the sick people who would need him and not find him, thinking how gently he took his short moments of pleasure without rebelling when they were interrupted. Thinking how deep his pleasure was in curing illness. Think-

93

ing how he had tried to control the drug traffic and refused to dispense dangerous forgetfulness. Thinking of his nights spent in studying drugs for remembrance, which were known to the Indians. As a port doctor, what underworld had he known which neither Lillian nor his wife could ever have known, but which his wife had sensed as dangerous.

Lillian was helping the wife up the hill, helping the woman who had hated the city he loved, and whose hatred was now justified by events.

"I have to prepare the children, but they are so young. What can I say to such young children about death?"

Lillian did not want to know whether he had bled, been cut by glass. It semed to her that he alone knew how to bandage, how to stop bleeding, how to heal.

The siren of the ambulance grew fainter. People walked behind them in silence.

If it were true that what we practice on others is secretly what we wish practiced upon ourselves, then he had wanted, needed all the care he gave.

To the wife with her too-high heels, her coiled black hair, her dark and jealous eyes, her small hands and feet, what could he have confided when from the beginning she turned against the city and the sick people he loved?

Lillian did not believe in the death of Doctor Hernandez, and yet she heard the shot, she felt in her body the sound of the car hitting the pole, she knew the moment of death, as if all of them had happened to her.

He had something to say, which he had not said, and he had left taking with him his secrets.

If only Doctor Hernandez had not postponed that deeper, wilder talk which ran underground through the myths of dreams, shouted through architectural crevices, screamed eloquently through the eyes of statues, from the depths of all the ancient cities within ourselves, if he had not merely signaled distress like a deaf-mute . . . . if only awareness had not appeared through the interstices of mem-

94

ory, between bars of lights and bars of shadows . . . if only human beings did not draw the blinds, don disguises, and live in isolation cells marked: not yet time for revelations . . . . if only they had gone down together, down the caverns of the soul with picks, lanterns, cords, oxygen, X-rays, food, following the blueprints of all the messages from the geological depths where lay hidden the imprisoned self . . . .

According to the definition, tropic meant a turning and changing, and with the tropics Lillian turned and changed, and she swung between the drug of forgetfulness and the drug of awareness, as the natives swung in their hammocks, as the jazz players swung into their rhythms, as the sea swung in its bed

turned
changed

Lillian was journeying homeward.

The other travelers were burdened with Mexican baskets, sarapes, shawls, silver jewelry, painted clay figurines and Mexican hats.

Lillian carried no objects, because none of them would have incarnated what she was bringing back, the softness of the atmosphere, the tenderness of the voices, the caressing colors and the whispering presence of an underworld of memory which had serpentined under her every footstep and which was the past she had not been able to forget. Her husband and her children had traveled with her. Had she not loved Larry in the prisoner she had liberated? Her first image of Larry had been of him standing behind a garden iron grille, watching her dance. He was the only one of her fellow students she had forgotten to invite to her eigh-

95

teenth birthday party. He had stood with his hands on the railing as the prisoner had stood in the Mexican jail, and she had seen him as a prisoner of his own silence and self-effacement. It was Larry and not the fraudulent prisoner she had wanted to liberate. Had she not loved her own children in Edwards' children, kissed Lietta's freckles because they were Adele's freckles, sat up with them evenings because their loneliness was her children's loneliness?

She was bringing back new images of her husband Larry, as if while she were away, some photographer with a new chemical had made new prints of the old films in which new aspects appeared she had never noticed before. As if a softer Lillian, who had absorbed some of the softness of the climate, some of the relaxed grace of the Mexicans, some of their genius for happiness had felt her senses sharpened, her vision more focused, her hearing more sensitive. As the inner turmoil quieted, she saw others more clearly. A less rebellious Lillian had become aware that when Larry was not there she had either become him or had looked for him in others.

If she had not talked to Doctor Hernandez it was because he had been seeking to bring to the surface what he knew to be her incompletely drowned marriage.

Doctor Hernandez. As she sat in the airplane, she saw him bending over his doctor's bag unrolling bandages. She could not reconstruct his face. He turned away from her because she had not given him the confidence he asked for. This fleeting glimpse of him appeared as if on glass, and vanished, dissolved in the sun.

Diana had told Lillian just before she left: I believe I know the real cause of his death. He felt alone, divided from his wife, dealing only in the casual, intermittent friendships with people who changed every day. It was not a bullet which killed him. He was too deeply trained to combat death, to consider death as a private enemy, to accept suicide. But he brought it about in such a roundabout way, in so subtle a way that he could delude himself that he had no hand in his own death. HE COULD HAVE AVOIDED THE CONFLICT WITH THE DRUG SMUGGLERS. It was not his responsibility. He could have left this task to the police, better equipped to handle them. Something impelled him to seek danger, to challenge these violent men. ALMOST TO INVITE THEM TO KILL HIM. I often warned him, and he would smile. I knew what was truly killing him: an accumulation of defeats, the knowledge that even his wife loved in him the doctor and not the man. Did you know that she had been near death when they met, that he had cured her, and that even after their marriage it was his care of others that she was jealous of? To you he may have seemed beloved, but in his own eyes all the love went to the man with the miraculous valise. Golconda was a place for fluctuating friendships, so many strangers passing through for a few days. Once he reproached me bitterly for my mobility and flexibility.

"You never hang on," he said, "this constant flow suits your fickle temperament. But I would like something deeper and more permanent. The more gayety there is around me, the more alone I feel."

And Lillian must have added to his feeling. She had failed to give him that revelation of herself which he had wanted, a gift which might have enabled him to confide too. He was suffering from denials she had not divined. And how tired he must have been of people's disappearances. They came to Golconda, they sat at the beach with him, they had dinner with him, they talked with him for the length of a consultation, and then left for other countries. What a relief it may have been to have become at last the one who left!

Diana was certain that he had subtly sought out his death. And now to this image Lillian could add others which until now had not fitted in. The image of his distress magnetized a series of impressions caught at various times

97

but abandoned like impressionistic fragments which did not coagulate. The shutters of the eyes opening to reveal anxiety, discouragement, solitude, all the more somber by contrast with the landscape of orange, turquoise, and gold. He had seemed to flow with all the life currents of Golconda. She had accepted only the surface evidence. But the selves of Doctor Hernandez which had lived in the periphery, backstage, now emerged unexpectedly. And with them all the invisible areas of life, his and hers, and others', which the eyes of the psyche sees but which the total self refuses to acknowledge, when at times these "ghosts" contain the living self and it is the personage on the stage who is empty and somnambulistic. It was as if having begun to see the true Doctor Hernandez, solitary, estranged from his wife and his children by her jealousy and hatred of Golconda immersed only in the troubled, tragic life of a pleasure city, she could also see for the first time, around the one dimensional profile of her husband, a husband leaving for work, a father bending over his children, an immense new personality. It was Larry, the prisoner of his own silences which she had liberated the day she visited the fraululent one in jail. It was Larry's silent messages she had been able to read through the bars of the Mexican jail. Once the vision becomes dual, or triple, like those lens which fracture the designs one turns them on but also repeats them to infinity in varied arrangements, she could see at least two Larrys, one bearing an expression of hunger and longing which had penetrated her the day of her birthday party more deeply than the gayety of her dancing partners, the other as the kind father and husband who dispensed care and gifts and tenderness perhaps as Doctor Hernandez had done, while desiring some unattainable pleasure.

Another image of Larry which appeared through the thick glass window of the plane, was of him standing behind the glass partition of a television studio. Lillian had been playing with an orchestra for a recording and Larry had sat in the recording room. He had forgotten that she could not hear him, and when the music had ended had stood up and talked, smiling and gesturing, in an effort to convey his enthusiasm for the music. The perplexed expression of her face urged him to magnify his gestures, to exaggerate the expression of his face, to dramatize beyond his usual manner, hoping that by a mime of his entire body and face he could transmit a message without the help of words.

At the time the scene had been baffling to Lillian, but only today did she understand it. She had failed to hear Larry, because he did not employ the most obvious means of communication. These two images seemed like a condensation of the drama of their marriage. First her response to his mute needs, his mute calling to her, and then her failure to captate his message. He had been a prisoner of his own silences, and these silences she had interpreted as absences.

He had answered her needs! What she had required of love was something that should never be expected of a human being, a love so strong that it might neutralize her self-disparagement, a love that would be occupied day and night with the reconstruction of a lovable Lillian, an image she would tear down as quickly as he created it. A love of such mathematical precision, occupied in keeping in inward balance between her self-caricature and a Lillian she might accept. A love tirelessly repeating: Lillian you are beautiful, Lillian you are wonderful, Lillian you are generous, and kind, and inspiring, while she, on the other side of the ledger made her own entries: Lillian, you are unjustly angry, you were thoughtless, you hurt someone's feelings, you were not patient with your child.

Endless accounting, endless revising of accounts.

But what had Larry wanted? It was true that Larry had accepted this abdication from life and seemed fulfilled when she lived for him in the musicians' world (because he had first wanted to be a musician, and had not fulfilled

99

this wish). It was true that he seemed content in his silences, content to let her and her jazz musicians play and talk. This peripheral life seemed natural to him. But this division of labor had become a charade. When they grew tired of it (Lillian tired of Larry's indirect spectatorships, and Larry tired of Lillian's predominant role) they had not known how to exchange roles! Larry began to crystallize, not having any direct flow into life, not having his own aqualungs, his own oxygen. They were like twins with one set of lungs. And all Lillian knew was to sustain the flow by escaping into other lives a movement which gave her the illusion of a completed circle. No other relationship could complete her, for it was Larry she had wanted to share life with, and ultimately she was seeking Larry in the other personages.

This last voyage without him had confronted her with her own incompleteness. She had deluded herself that the lungs, the capacity to live, were hers alone. How much of Larry she had carried within herself and enacted as soon as he was not there to act it for her. It was she who did not talk then, who let the Mexicans talk nimbly and flowingly, as she let Doctor Hernandez monologue. It was she who had remained at a distance from the life of Golconda except for the moment of abandon to the lulling drugs of nature. She had behaved as Larry would have behaved. Her courage, her flow in life had only existed in relation to Larry, by comparison with his withdrawals. What had he done while deprived of her presence? Probably had lived out the Lillian he carried within himself, her traits. Towards what Larry was she voyaging now?

Was it not an act of love to impersonate the loved one? Was it not like the strange "possessions" which take place at the loss of a parent by death? When her mother died, Lillian *became* her mother for at least a long year of mourning. It had been an imperceptible possession, for Lillian did not belong to the race who had rituals at which these truths were dramatized, rituals at which the spirit of the "departed"

100

entered the body of the living, at which the spirit of the dead parent was acknowledge to be capable of entering the body of the son or daughter and inhabit until driven, or prayed, or chased away. To all appearances these primitive beliefs and what happened to Lillian were not related. Yet the spirit of her mother had passed into her. When she died, leaving Lillian a thimble, and a sewing machine (when Lillian could not sew) Lillian did not know that she took on some of her moods, characteristics, attitudes. She once thought it was that as one grew older one had less resistance to the influences of the family and one surrendered to family resemblances.

Lillian laughed at the primitive rituals of "possession" she had seen in Haiti. But there was a primitive Lillian who had combated the total loss of her mother by a willingness to take into herself some of her mannerisms and traits (the very ones she had rebelled against while her mother was alive, the very ones which had injured her own growth). It was not only that she began to sew, to use the thimble and the sewing machine, but that she began to whistle when her children strayed from the house, she scolded her children for the very traits her mother had censured in her: neglect in dress, impulsive, chaotic behaviour. A strange way to erect a monument to the memory of her mother, a monument to her continuity.

Thus she had also been "possessed" by Larry, and it was his selectivity in people which spoke against Diana's lack of discrimination. For the first time, in Golconda, she had practised Larry's choice of withdrawing if the people were not of quality. Of preferring solitude to the effort of pretending he was interested in them.

Nearing home, she wondered if both of them had not accepted roles handed to them by others' needs as conditions of the marriage. It was the need which had dictated the role. And roles dictated by a need and not the whole self caused a withering in time. They had been married to

101

parts of themselves only. Just as Dr. Hernandez had married a woman who loved only the Doctor, and who never knew the man who had tried to shed his role by entering the violent world of the smugglers, to feel himself in the heart of life, even at the cost of death.

Lillian had felt responsible for the Doctor's death, but now she knew it was not a personal responsibility; it was because she too had lived with only a part of Larry, and when you live with only a part of a person, you symbolically condemn the rest of it to indifference, to oblivion.

She knew it was not a bullet which had killed Dr. Hernandez. He had placed himself in the bullet's path. Certainly at times his intelligence and knowledge of human nature must have warned him that he was courting sudden death when he refused to surrender his supply of drugs or to underwrite fake permits to obtain more.

She knew that by similar detours of the labyrinth, it was not the absence of love or the death of it which had estranged her from Larry, but the absence of communication between all the parts of themselves, the sides of their character which each one feared to uncover in the other. The channels of emotions were just like the passageways running through our physical body which some illness congests, and renders narrower and narrower until the supply of oxygen and blood is diminished and brings on death. The passageways of their communication with each other had shrunk. They had singled out their first image of each other as if they had selected the first photograph of each other, to live with forever, regardless of change or growth. They had set it upon their desks, and within their hearts, a photograph of Larry as he had first appeared behind the garden gate, mute and hungry, and a photograph of Lillian in distress because her faith in herself had been killed by her parents.

If they had been flowing together in life, they would not have created these areas of vacuum into which other relationships had penetrated, just as if Doctor Hernandez had been loved and happy in Golconda, he would have found a way to escape his enemies. (Diana had proofs that he had been warned, offered help, and recklessly disregarded both).

The manner in which Lillian had finally immured herself against the life in Golconda betrayed how she, as well as Larry, often closed doors against experience, and lived by patterns.

Diana had said: "People only called him when they were in distress. When they gave parties they never thought of him. I knew that what he gave to others was what he deeply wanted for himself. This sympathy . . . for those in trouble. I do believe he was in greater trouble than any of us."

His death set in motion a chain of disappearances, an awareness of the dangers of disappearances. And this fear fecundated Lillian, stirred all life and feeling into bloom again. Sudden death had exposed the preciousness of human love and human life. All the negations, withdrawals, indifferences seemed like the precursors of absolute death, and were to be condemned. She had a vision of a world without Larry and without her children, and then she knew that her love of Golconda had only been possible because of the knowledge that her absence was temporary.

And now the words spoken by Doctor Hernandez were clear to her, their meaning reached her. "We may seem to forget a person, a place, a state of being, a past life, but meanwhile what we are doing is selecting new actors, seeking the closest reproduction to the friend, the lover, the husband we are trying to forget, in order to re-enact the drama with understudies. And one day we open our eyes and there we are, repeating the same story. How could it be otherwise. The design comes from within us. It is internal. It is what the old mystics described as karma, repeated until the spiritual or emotional experience was understood, liquidated, achieved."

All the personages had been there, not to be described

103

in words but by a series of images. The prisoner had touched her only because he vaguely echoed the first image of Larry as he appeared behind the iron gate. Even if this prisoner had been fraudulent, his acting had been good enough to re-awaken in Lillian her feelings towards the first Larry she had known, a Larry in trouble, a trouble which she deeply shared, was married to, not only by empathy but by affinity. She had disguised it by throwing herself into life and relationships, by appearing fearless and passionate, and it had taken the true freedom of Golconda, its fluid, soft, flowing life, to expose her own imprisonment, her own awkwardness. She had been more mated to Larry than she had known. She had been as much afraid, only fear had made her active, leaping and courting and loving and giving and seeking, but driven by the same fear which made Larry recoil into his home and solitude. In losing this first intuitive knowledge she had of the bond between them, she had also lost a truth about herself. She had been taken in by the myth of her courage, the myth of her warmth and flow. And it was the belief in this myth which had caused her to pass judgment on the static quality of Larry, concealing the static elements in herself.

One night Doctor Hernandez, Fred, Diana and Edward had decided to visit the native dance halls of Golconda which opened on small, unpaved streets behind the market. They leaped across an open trench of sewer water, on to a dirt floor, and sat at a table covered with a red oil-cloth. Tropical plants growing out of gasoline cans partly veiled them from the street. Red bulbs strung on wires cast charcoal shadows and painted the skins in the changing tones of leaping flames. A piano out of tune gave out a sound of broken glass. The drums always dominated the melodies, whether songs or jute boxes, insistent like the drums of Africa. The houses being like gardens with roofs, the various musics mingled, guitars, a Cuban dance orchestra, a woman's voice. But the dancers obeyed the drums.

The skins matched all the tones of chocolate, coffee and wood. There were many white suits and dresses, and many of those flowered dresses which in the realm of printed dresses stand in the same relation as the old paintings of flowers and fruit done by maiden aunts to a Matisse, or a Braque. They had been unwilling to separate themselves from their daily fare in food, the daily appearance of a dining table.

All the people she had seen in Golconda were there: taxi drivers, policemen, shopkeepers, truck drivers, life savers, beach photographers, lemon vendors, and the owner of the glass bottom boat. The men danced with the prostitutes of Golconda, and these were the girls Lillian had seen sewing quietly at windows, selling fruit at the market, and they brought to their evening profession the same lowered eyes, gentle voices, and passive quietude. They were dressed more enticingly, showed more shoulders and arms, but not provocatively. It was the men who drank and raised their voices. The policemen had tied their gun halters to their chairs.

The natives danced in bare feet, and Lillian kicked off her sandals. The dirt floor was warm and dry, and just as the night she had danced on the beach with the sea licking her toes, she felt no interruption between the earth and her body as if the same sap and rhythm ran through both simultaneously, gold, green, watery, or fiery when you touched the core.

Everyone spoke to Doctor Hernandez. Even tottering drunk, they bowed with respect.

A singer was chanting the Mexican plainsong, a lamentation on the woes of passion. Tequila ran freely, sharpened by lemon and salt on the tongue. The voices grew husky and the figures blurred. The naked feet trampled the dirt, and the bodies lost their identities and flowed into a single dance, moved by one beat. The heat from the bowels of the earth warmed their feet.

105

Doctor Hernandez frowned and said: "Lillian, put your sandals on!" His tone was protective; she knew he could justify this as a grave medical counsel. But she felt fiercely rebellious at anyone who might put an end to this magnetic connection with others, with the earth, and with the dance, and with the messages of sensuality passing between them.

With Fred too, she was unaccountably angry. Because he looked pale and withdrawn, and because he was watching, not entering. He kept his shoes on, and not even the monodic jubilance of the singer could dissolve this peregrine, this foreign visitor. And then it was not longer Fred who sat there, spectator and fire extinguisher, but all those who had been an obstacle to her efforts to touch the fiery core.

The plants which overflowed into the dance hall and brushed the shoulders, uninvited guests from the jungle, the sharp stinging scent of tequila, the milk of cactus, the cries of the street like the cries of animals in the forest, bird, monkey, the burning eyes of the urchins watching through the leaves almost as phosphorescent as the eyes of wildcats; the water of the sewers running through the trench hissing like a fountain, the taxis throwing their headlights upon the dancers, beacons of a tumultuous sea of the senses, the perspiration on the shirt backs, the touch of toes more intimate than the touch of hands, the round tables seeming to turn like ouija boards of censurable messages, every message a caress, all this orchestration of the effulgence of the tropics served to measure by contrast these moments of existence which did not bloom completely, moments lived dimly, conjunctions and fusions which did not take place.

Larry and she had touched at one point, caught a glimpse of their undisguised self, but had not fused completely. Poor receptivity, poor connections, and at times no contact at all. Lillian knew now that it was an illusion that one lived in full possession of one's body. It could slip away

106

from one. She could see Fred achieving this by impermeability to the sensuality of the place and people.

"Put your sandals on!" repeated Doctor Hernandez, and Lillian translated it: he wanted to protect her from promiscuity. That had been his role. She must defy him from causing more short circuits, more disconnections. And she must defy Fred, who, as in those dreams in which the identity is not clear, became all the ones who had not answered her love and particularly the first one, Gerard. When Fred danced with her, clumsily, soberly, she looked down at his boots as a sign of deliberate insulation, and she pushed him away and said: "your shoes hurt me."

The time was past when her body could be ravished from her by visitations from the world of guilt. Such pleasurable sensations as a kiss on the inside of her arm, in the nook within the elbow, given by a stranger at a dance had been enough at one time to cause sudden departures. But no one could break now her feeling of oneness with Golconda. She had betrayed Larry with all the voluptuous textures, pungent smells and with pleasure.

The girls had noticed that Lillian would not dance with Fred, and they came to sit at his side. One of them wore a black satin dress with an edge of white lace which seemed like a petticoat making an indiscreet appearance. The other a shawl which was slipped off her shoulders constantly as by an invisible hand. One had the expression of a schoolgirl intent upon her work. Her hair was still damp from the beach, and hung straight down like a Tahitian's. The other smiled and rested a fine boned, delicate, small hand upon Fred's knees. Then she leaned over and still smiling, whispered in his ear a request which made the blood rush to Fred's face, and his body stiffen with panic. The girl on his left, her small earrings trembling, and her medal of the Virgin engraved in blue lacquer which she held between her fingers like a cigarette, added: "The two of us? More exciting?"

Fred threw a distressed glance at Lillian, who was laughing. One girl was kissing the lobe of his ear, and the other slipping her hand inside his shirt.

"Lillian, help me."

He could not extricate himself. He had seen them at the beach, selling shells, fish, lace. He had seen them entering the church, with black veils over their hair.

Seeing the depth of his distress, Lillian said: "Let's go swimming. It's too hot to dance anymore." It was true: their clothes were glued to their bodies, and their hair looked as if they had been swimming.

The girls clung to Fred: "You stay," they said.

Lillian leaned over to them and said in Spanish: "Some other night. Tonight he feels he must stay with me."

Their hands fell off his shoulders.

Now they were in a taxi, joggling over dirt roads.

Fred did not know that during the evening he had lost his identity in Lillian's eyes and become Gerard, her first defeat at the hands of passivity. A Gerard whose paralysis she now recognized and no longer desired. One could not lust for a wall, an obstacle, an inert mass, yet she had once been seduced by just such gentleness and passivity. It had calmed her fears. She did not know then what she knew now: it had been an encounter with a fear greater than her own. She could desire him violently (Gerard) because she had an instinctive knowledge that he would not respond. She could desire him without restraint (and even admire her own spontaneity) because the restraint was safely prearranged within him. She was free to desire knowing that she would not be swept away into any fusion. It seemed absurd to say that one would refuse a glass of water when one was thirsty, *but if this glass of water also represented all the dangers of love?* When Lillian was sixteen or seventeen, fulfilment itself was the danger, love itself was the danger, a shared passion was slavery. She would be at the mercy of another human being. (Just as Fred now feared to be at

108

the mercy of a woman). Whereas by desiring someone who would not desire her, she could allow this fire to burn and feel: how alive I am! I am capable of desire. Poor Gerard, what a coward he is. He is afraid of life. It was not, as she thought, the pain of being alive she felt, but the pain of frustration.

How elated she was now not to have been seduced by Fred's mute pleadings and his retractions. How grateful to have discovered not a failed love affair, but the secret of that failure to lie in the choice of partner, a choice which came out of fear. So it was fear who had designed her life, and not desire or love.

If they did not arrive too soon at the secret cove known only to Doctor Hernandez, she would have time to make inevitable deductions. She and Larry had selected each other and each had played the role which kept their fears from overwhelming them. How could they pass judgment on each other for playing the role they had assigned to each other? You, Larry, must not change, or move, must represent fixed, unalterable love. You, Lillian, must change and move for both to sustain the myth of freedom.

Fred was afraid of the night, afraid of Diana who was cooling her body by pulling her dress out away from her breasts, waving it before her like a fan, he was afraid of Lillian who was fanning her face with the edge of her cotton dress, exposing the lacy petticoat.

The taxi left them at the top of the hill, and Doctor Hernandez guided them through brambles and rocks, down hill, to his secret cove.

Fred was afraid of the night, afraid his body would slip away from him, dissolve in that purple velvet with diamond eyes, the tropical night. The tropical night did not lie inert, like a painted movie backdrop, but was filled with whisperings, and seemed to have arms like the foliage.

Beauty was a drug. The small beach shone like mercury at their feet. They undressed in the rocks which formed a cavern. The waves absorbed the words, one only heard the laughter or a name. Diana, painted by the moonlight walked like a phosphorescent Venus into the waves. The oil lamps on the fishermen's small boats trembled like candlelight. The neon lights softened by the haze threw beams on the bay like miniature searchlights.

Fred was as troubled as if he had encountered the singing mermaids. He did not undress. Doctor Hernandez swam far out, he was familiar with every rock. Lillian and Edward stayed near the shore. The fatigue and the heat of the dance were washed away. The sea swung like a hammock. One could grow a new skin over the body. The undulations of the sea were like their breathing, as if the sea and the swimmers had but one lung.

Out of the full beauty of the tropical night, the full moon, the full bloom of the stars, the full velvet of the night, a full woman might be born. No more scattered fragments of herself living separate cellular lives, living at times in the temporary home of others' lives.

Fred stood further away, clinging to his locks and his clocks, to peripheries, islands, bridges. The taxi driver smoked a cigarette and was singing the melopeia of love.

Fred's immobility, sitting by the rock, not sharing in the baptismal immersion, gave birth to an image of Larry's absence of mobility. But as the psyche changes, it recreates semantics, and the word "fixity" had once been considered a virtue. It was this fixity she had summoned, needed, loved, because in her chaos and confusions, fixity was the symbol of immutability, eternity. An unchanging love. How unjust to change its meaning when this unchanging love had been the hot house in which she had been born as a woman. Was it possible to begin one's life anew with a knowledge of what lay behind the charades one had created? Would she circumvent the masks they had donned, those she had pinned upon the face of Larry? She now knew her responsibility in the symbolic drama of their marriage.

110

Lillian was journeying homeward. The detours of the labyrinth did not expose disillusion, but unexplored dimensions. Archeologists of the soul never returned empty handed. Lillian had felt the existence of the labyrinth beneath her feet like the excavated passageways under Mexico City, but she had feared entering it and meeting the Minotaur who would devour her.

Yet now that she had come face to face with it, the Minotaur resembled someone she knew. It was not a monster. It was a reflection upon a mirror, a masked woman, Lillian herself, the hidden masked part of herself unknown to her, who had ruled her acts. She extended her hand toward this tyrant who could no longer harm her. It lay upon the mirror of the plane's round portholes, traveling through the clouds, a fleeting face, her own, clear and definable only when darkness came.

Even though the airplane was taking her back to White Plains after an engagement of three months in Golconda, a little girl of six running up and down the aisle of the plane carried her by a detour into the past, to a certain day in her childhood, in Mexico, where her father frustrated by enigmatic natives, and elemental cataclysms, would come home to the one kingdom, at least, where his will was unquestioned. He would receive from the mother a report on the day. And no matter how mild she made this, how much she attenuated the children's infractions, the father always found the cause enough to march them up to the top floor, an attic filled with dusty objects. And there, one by one, he spanked them.

As the rest of the time he did not talk to them, nor play with them nor cuddle them, nor sing to them, nor read to them, as he acted in fact as if they were not there, this moment in the attic produced in Lillian two distinct emotions: one of humiliation, the other the pleasure of intimacy. As there were no other moments of intimacy with her father Lillian began to regard the attic as a place which was both the scene of spankings but also of the only rite shared with her father. For years, in telling of it, she only stressed the injustice, the ignominy of it. She stressed how there came a day when she openly rebelled and frightened her father into giving up this punishment.

But once in Paris, she strayed into an Arcade and saw people watching penny movies with such delight and interest that she waited her turn and slipped a penny in a slot. A little movie scene appeared, awkward and jerky like the movies of the 1920's. A family sat at dinner, father (with a mustache) mother in a ruffled dress, and three children. The young and pretty maid was serving the soup. She was dressed in black. Her dress was very short. It revealed a white lace edged petticoat, and she wore a butterfly of white lace on her hair. She spilled the soup on the father's lap. The father rose in a fury, and left the table to go and change his clothes. The maid had not only to help him change his clothes, but to atone for the accident.

Lillian was about to leave, unmoved, amused, when the machine clicked and a new film began. The scene this time took place in a classroom. The students were little girls of six or seven (Lillian's age when she was receiving the spankings). They were dressed in old-fashioned frilly and bouffant dresses. The teacher was angered by their mockeries and laughter, and asked them to come up, one by one, to be spanked (just as Lillian and her sisters and brothers were lined up and made to march up the stairs). At this scene Lillian's heart began to beat wildly. She thought she was about to relive the pain and humiliation caused by her father.

But when the teacher lifted up the little girl, stretched her across his knees, turned up her skirt, pulled down her panties, and began to spank her what Lillian experienced after twenty years was not pain, but a flooding joy of sensual excitement. As if the spankings, while hurting her, had been at the same time the only caress she had known from

112

her father. Pain had become inextricably mixed with joy at his presence, the distorted closeness had alchemized into pleasure. The rite, intended as a punishment, had become the only intimacy she had known, the only contact, a substitution of anger and tears in place of tenderness.

She wanted to be in the little girl's place!

She hurried away from the Arcade, trembling with joy, as if she were returning from an erotic adventure.

Thus the real dictator, the organizer and director of her life had been this quest for a chemical compound—so many ounces of pain mixed with so many ounces of pleasure in a formula known only to the unconscious. The failure lay in the enormous difference between the relationship she had needed, and the one she had, on a deeper level, more deeply wanted. The need was created out of an aggregate of negativities and deformations. When Lillian thought that in her relationship to Jay she was only in bondage to a passion, she was also in bondage to a need. When she thought her stays in Paris were directed entirely by a desire for Jay, they were in fact pre-determined on those days in Mexico when she was six or seven years old.

Not enough of that measure of pain had existed in her marriage to Larry.

In the laboratories the scientists were trying to isolate the virus which might be the cause of cancer. Djuna believed one could isolate the virus which destroys love. But then there were outcries: that this would be the end of illusion, when it was only the beginning! Lillian had learned from Djuna that each cell, once separated from the diseased one, was capable of new life.

Erasing the grooves. It was not that Lillian nad remained attached to the father, and incapable of other attachments. It was that the form of the relationship, the mould, had become a groove, the groove itself was familiar, her footsteps followed it habitually, unquestioningly, the familiar groove of pain and pleasure, of closeness at the cost of pain.

Lillian remembered Djuna's words: Man is not falling apart. He *is* undergoing a kind of fission, but I believe in those who are trying quietly to isolate the destructive cells, so that after fission each part is illumined and alive, waiting for a new fusion.

Was this why Lillian had always wept at weddings? Had she known obscurely that each human being might lie wrapped in his self-created myth, in the first plaster cast made by his emotions. Static and unchangeable, each could move only in the grooves etched by the past.

Jay had appeared at first as the bearer of joy, she had loved his complete union with the earth, his acceptance of the hungry, the greedy animal within himself. He lived with blinkers on, seeking only pleasure, avoiding responsibilities and duties, swimming skilfully on the surface, enjoying, suspicious of depths, out in the world, preferring the many to the few, intoxication with life only, wherever it carried him, not faithful to individuals, or to ideas. Seeking the flow, the living moment only. Never looking back or looking into the future.

His talk of violence suited her tumultuous nature. But then he had made love without violence, and then asked her: did you expect more brutality? She did not know this man. The first room he had taken her to was shabby. He had said: look how worn the carpet is. But all she could see was the golden glow, the sun behind the curtain. All she could hear were his words: Lillian, your eyes are full of wonder. You expect a miracle every day. His brown shirt hung behind the door, there was only one glass to drink from and a mountain of sketches and note books she was to sort out later, silk screen and arrange into the famous Portfolio. He had no time to stop. There was too much to see in the streets. He had just discovered the Algerian street,

114

with its smell of saffron, and the Algerian melopeia issuing from dark medieval doorways.

Lillian felt they would live out something new. They had first known each other in New York, when Lillian was disconnected from Larry. Jay had left for Paris because he wanted to live near the painters he admired. Lillian's engagement took her there for several months each year. New for her, this total acceptance of all life, ugliness, poverty, sensuality, Jay's total acceptance, lack of selectivity or discrimination or withdrawals. Lillian thought him a gentle savage, a passionate cannibal. Motherhood prepared Lillian for this abdication of herself. Lillian adopted all his infatuations and enthusiasms: she sat with him contemplating from a cafe table the orange face of a clock, the prostitute with the wooden leg; played chess at the Cafe de La Regence at the very table where Napoleon and Robespierre had played chess. She helped him gather and note fifty ways of saying drunk.

She abandoned classical music and became a jazz pianist. Classical music could not contain her improvisations, her tempo, her vehemences.

She watched over Jay's work, searched Paris shops for the best paint, even learned to make some from ancient crafts. She watched over his needs. She had his sketch book silk screened and carried the Portfolios to New York and sold them. People were asking questions about Jay. They laughed at his casual gifts to them, loved the freedom, the unbound pages, the surprises, which gave them the feeling they were sharing an intimate, private document, like a personal sketch book.

His rooms remained the same everywhere, the plain iron bed, the hard pillows, the one glass. They were illumined by orgies: let us see how long we can make love, how long, how many hours, days, nights.

When she went to New York to visit her children, he wrote to her: "Terribly alive but pained, and feeling absolutely that I need you. But I must see you soon. I see you bright and wonderful. I want to get more familiar with you. I love you. I loved you when you came and sat on the edge of the bed. All that afternoon like warm mist. Get closer to me, I promise you it will be beautiful. I like so much your frankness, your humility almost. I could never hurt that. It was to a woman like you I should have been married."

Small room, so shabby, like a deep-set alcove. Immediately there was the richness of Jay's voice, the feeling of sinking into warm flesh, every twist of the body awakening new centers of pleasure. Everything is good, good, murmured Jay. Have I been less brutal than you expected? Did the violence of my painting lead you to expect more? Lillian was baffled by these questions. What was he measuring himself against? A myth in his own mind of what women expected?

In his own work everything was larger than nature. Was he trying to match his own extravagances? If in his eyes he carried magnifying glasses, did he see himself in life as a smaller figure?

In the same letter he wrote: "I don't know what I expect of you, Lillian, but it is something in the way of a miracle. I am going to demand everything of you, even the impossible, because you are strong."

Lillian's secret weakness then became the cause of pain. She had a need of a mirror, in which she could see her image loved by Jay. Or perhaps a shrine, with herself in the place of honor. Unique and irreplaceable Lillian (as she had been for Larry). But with Jay this was impossible. The whole world flowed through his being in one day. Lillian was apt to find sitting in her place (or lying in her bed) the most unlovely of all women, undernourished, unkempt, anonymous, ordinary, he had picked up in a cafe, with nothing to explain her presence except that she was perhaps the opposite of Lillian. To her he gave the coat Lillian had left in his room. The visitor had even brought with her a little grey wilted dog and Jay who hated animals was even kind to this dusty mongrel that was moulting.

For Jay's kindness was his greatest expression of anarchy. It was always an act of defiance to those one loved, to those one lived with. His was a mockery of the laws of devotion. He could not give to Lillian. He was always generous to outsiders, to those he owed nothing to, giving paints to those who did not paint, a drink to the man who was oversaturated with drink, his time to one who did not value it, the painting Lillian favored to anyone who came to the studio.

His giving was a defiance of evaluation and selection. He wanted to assert the value of what others discarded or neglected. His favorite friend was not a great painter but the most mediocre of all painters, who reflected Jay like a caricature, a diminished echo, who hummed his words as Jay did, nodded his head as Jay did, laughed when Jay laughed. They practised dadaism together: everything was absurd, everything was a joke. Jay would launch into frenzied praise of his paintings. (Lillian called him Sancho Panza.)

Lillian would ask with candor: "Do you really admire him so much, as much as all that? Is he truly greater than Gauguin? Greater than Picasso?"

Jay would laugh at her gravity. "Oh, no, I was carried away by my own words, just got going. I think I was talking about my own painting, really. I enjoy mystifying, confusing, contradicting. Deep down, you know, I don't believe in anything."

"But people will believe you."

"They admire the wrong painters anyway."

"But you're adding to the absurdities."

Lillian had the feeling that Sancho did not exist. True he presented a Chinese face, but when she sought to know Sancho she found an evasive smile which was a reflection of Jay's smile, a sympathy which was an act of politeness, an

opinion which at the slightest opposition, vanished, a head
waiter at a banquet, a valet for your coat, a shadow at the
top of the stairs. His eyes carried no messages. If her
fingers touched him she felt his body was fluid, evasive,
anonymous. What Jay asserted he did not deny. He imi-
tated Jay's adventures but Lillian felt he had neither possessed life, nor lost it, neither devoured it nor spat it out. He
was the wool in the bedroom slipper, the storm strip on the
window, the felt stop on the piano key, the shock absorber
on the car spring. He was the invisible man, and Lillian
could not understand their fraternal bond. She suffered to
see a reduced replica of Jay, his shrunken double.

"Right after being with me," Lillian said once, "did
you have to take up with such an unlovely woman?"

"Oh, that," said Jay. "Reichel believes me to be callous,
amoral, ungrateful. He thinks because I have you I'm the
luckiest man in the world, and it irritated me, his lecturing,
so I launched into a role, to shock him. I talked to him about
the whores, and had him gasping to think I might be callous
about you. Can you understand that? I realize that it's all
childish, but don't take it seriously."

"Eh? Sancho?" Sancho would laugh hysterically. It
was what Lillian called the Village Idiot Act. Lillian laughed
with them, but not with all of herself.

"I'm finding my own world," said Jay. "A certain condition of existence, a universe of mere BEING, where one lives
like a plant, instinctively. No will. The great indifference,
like that of the Hindu who lets himself be passive in order
to let the seeds in him flower. Something between the will
of the European and the Karma of the oriental. I want just
the joy of illumination, the joy of what I see in the world.
Just to receive vibrations. Susceptibility to all life. Acceptance. Taking it all in. Just BE. That was always the
role of the artist, to reveal the joy, the ecstasy. My life has
been one long opposition to will. I have practised letting
things happen. I have dodged jobs, responsibilities, and I

118

want to express in painting the relaxing of will and straining for the sake of enjoyment."

This was the climate he created and to which Lillian responded, the yieldingness of the body, relaxed gestures, yielding to flow, seeking pleasure and being nourished with it, giving it to others. When something threatened his pleasure how skilful he was at evasion. He had created something which on the surface, seemed untainted by the anxiety of his time, yet Lillian felt there was a flaw in it. She did not know what it was.

The flaw, she was to discover that his world was like a child's world, depending on others' care, others' devotions, others' taking on the burdens.

He received a letter from his first wife, telling him about his daughter now fourteen years old, and showing exceptional gifts for painting. At first Jay wept: "I cannot help her." He remembered saying to her when she was five years old: "Now remember, I am your brother, not your father." The idea of fatherhood repulsed him. It threatened his desire for everlasting freedom and youthfulness.

"Let her come and share our life," said Lillian.

"No," said Jay. "I want to be free. I have too much work to do. I have to take the frames off my paintings. I want them to become a part of the wall, a continuous frieze. My colors are about to fly off the edge, and I don't want restraint. Let them fly!"

While Lillian cooked dinner in the small kitchen off the studio, he fell asleep. When he awakened he had forgotten his daughter and his guilt. "Is dinner ready? Is the wine good?"

How I wish his indifference were contagious, thought Lillian. He can forget his daughter, and I cannot forget my children. Every night I leave Jay's side to go and say goodnight to my children across the ocean. I have to give Jay the same kind of love I gave my children. As if I knew no other expression of love outside of care and devotion.

119

She spent all her time consoling the friends he had misused, paying his debts, preventing him from paying too high a price for his rebellions.

When they first met he was proofreading in a newspaper office. His paintings were not selling yet. The work irritated his eyes. He would come to his room and the first thing he would do was to wash his inflamed eyelids. Lillian watched him, watched the red-rimmed eyes, usually laughing, and now withered by fatigue, and watering. These eyes which he needed for his work, wasted on proofreading under weak lights on greyish paper. These eyes he needed to drink in the world and all its profusion of images.

"Jay," said Lillian, extending a glass of red wine. "Drink to the end of your job at the paper. You will never have to do it again. I earn enough for both of us when I play every night."

He had at times the air of a gnome, a satyr, or at other times the air of a serious scholar. His body appeared fragile in proportion to his exuberance. His appetite for life was enormous. His parents had given him money to go to college. He had put it in his pocket and gone to wander all over America, taking any job that came along, and sometimes none, travelling with hoboes, as a hitchhiker, a fruit picker, a dish washer, seeking adventure, enriching his experience. He did not see his parents again for many years. In one blow, he had severed himself from his childhood, his adolescence, from all his past.

What richness, Lillian felt, what a torrent. In a world chilled by the mind his work poured out like a volcano and raised the surrounding temperature.

"Lillian, let's drink to my Pissoir Period. I have been painting the joys of urinating. It's wonderful to urinate while looking up at the Sacre Coeur and thinking of Robinson Crusoe. Even better still in the urinoir of the Jardin des Plantes, while listening to the roar of the lions, and while the monkeys, high up in the trees, watch the performance and sometimes imitate me. Everything in nature is good."

He loved the boiling streets. While he walked the streets he was happy. He learned their names amorously as if they were the names of women. He knew them intimately, noted those which disappeared and those which were born. He took Lillian to the Rue d'Ulm which sounded like a poem by Edgar Allan Poe, to the Rue Feuillantine which sounded like a souffle of leaves, to the Quai de Valmy where the barges waited patiently in the locks for a change of level while the wives hung their laundry on the decks, watered their flower pots and ironed their lace curtains to make the barges seem more like a cottage in the country. Rue de la Fourche, like the trident of Neptune or of the devil, Rue Dolent with its mournful wall encircling the prison. Impasse du Mont Tonnerre! How he loved the Impasse du Mont Tonnerre. It was guarded at the entrance by a small cafe, three round tables on the sidewalk. A rusted iron gate which once opened to the entrance of carriages, now left open. A Hotel filled with Algerians who worked in a factory nearby. Rusty Algerian voices, monotone songs, shouts, spice smells, fatal quarrels, knife wounds.

Once having walked past the iron gate, over the uneven cobblestones, they entered the Middle Ages. Dogs were eating garbage, women were going to market in their bedroom slippers. An old concierge stared through half closed shutters, her skin the color of a mummy, a shrivelled mouth munching words he could not hear. "Who do you want to see?" The classical words of concierges. Jay answered: "Marat, Voltaire, Mallarme, Rimbaud."

"Every time I see one of those concierges," said Jay, "I am reminded of how in the Middle Ages they believed that a cat must be buried in the walls of a newly built house, it would bring luck. I feel that these are the cats come back to avenge themselves by losing your mail and misleading visitors."

121

Through an entrance as black and as narrow as the entrance to Mayan tombs, they entered gentle courtyards, with humble flower pots in bloom, cracked window one expected to be opened by Ninon de L'Enclos. The smallness of the window, the askewness of the frame, the hood of the grey pointed slate roof overhanging it had been painted so many times on canvas that it receded into the past, fixed, eternal, like the sea shell colored clouds suspended in time which could not be blown away by a change of wind.

Jay was sitting at the small coffee stained table like a hunter on the watch for adventure. Lillian said: "The painters and the writers heightened these places and those people so well that they seem more alive than today's houses, today's people. I can remember the words spoken by Leon Paul Fargue more than the words I hear today. I can hear the very sound of his restless cane on the pavement better than I can hear my own footsteps. Was their life as rich, as intense? Was it the artist who touched it up?"

Time and art had done for Suzanne Valadon, the mother of Utrillo, what Jay would never do for Sabina. Flavor by accretion, poetry by decantation. The artists of that time had placed their subject in a light which would forever entrance us, their love re-infected us. By the opposite process which he did not understand, but which he shared with many other artists of his time, he was conveying *his* inability to love. It was *his* hatred he was painting.

Jay once said: "I arrived by the same boat that takes the prisoners to Devil's Island. And I was thinking how strange it would be if I sailed back with them as a murderer. It was in Marseilles. I had picked up two girls in a cafe, and we were returning by taxi after a night of night clubs. One of the girls kept after me not to let myself get cheated. When we arrived at the Hotel the taxi driver asked me for a ridiculously high sum. I argued with him. I was very angry, and yet during that moment I was conscious that I was looking at his face with terrific intensity, as if I were going to kill him, but it was not that, my hatred was like a magnifying glass, taking in all the details, his porous meaty face, his moles with hair growing out of them, his soggy hair falling over his forehead, his cloudy eyes the color of Pernod. Finally we came to an agreement. That night I dreamed that I strangled him. The next day I painted him as I saw him in my dream. It was as if I had done it in reality. People will hate this painting."

"No, they will probably love it," said Lillian. "Djuna says that the criminal relieves others of their wish to commit murder. He acts out the crimes of the world. In your painting you depict the desire of thousands. In your erotic drawings you do the same. They will love your freedom."

At dawn they stood on the Place du Tertre, among houses which seemed about to crumble, to slide away, having been for so long the façades of Utrillo's houses.

Three policemen were strolling, watching. A street telephone rang hysterically in the vaporous dawn. The policemen began to run towards it.

"Someone committed your murder," said Lillian.

Two waiters and a woman began to run after the policemen. The loud ringing continued. One of the policemen picked up the telephone and to a question put to him he answered: "No, not at all, not at all. Don't worry. Everything is absolutely calm. A very calm night."

Lillian and Jay had sat on the curb and laughed.

But whatever Jay's secret of freedom was, it could not be imparted to Lillian. She could not gain it by contagion. All she could feel were Jay's secret needs: "Lillian, I need you. Lillian, be my guardian angel. Lillian, I need peace in which to work." Love, faithfulness, attentiveness, devotion, always created the same barriers around Lillian, the same limitations, the same taboos.

Jay avoided the moments of beauty in human beings. He stressed their analogies with animals. He added inert flesh, warts, oil to the hair, claws to the nails. He was sus-

123

picious of beauty. It was like a puritan's suspicion of make up, a crowd's suspicion of prestidigitators. He had divorced nature from beauty. Nature was neglect, unbuttoned clothes, uncombed hair, homeliness.

Lillian was bewildered by the enormous discrepancy which existed between Jay's models and what he painted. Together they would walk along the same Seine river, she would see it silky grey, sinuous and glittering, he would draw it opaque with fermented mud, and a shoal of wine bottle corks and weeds caught in the stagnant edges.

He had discovered a woman hobo who slept every night in exactly the same place, in the middle of the sidewalk, in front of the Pantheon. She had found a subway ventilator from which a little heat arose and sometimes a pale grey smoke, so that she seemed to be burning. She lay in a tidy way, her head resting on her market bag packed with her few belongings, her brown dress pulled over her ankles, her shawl neatly tied under her chin. She slept calm and dignified as if she were in her own bed. Jay had painted her soiled and scratched feet, the corn on her toes, the black nails. But he overlooked the story Lililan loved and remembered of her, that when they tried to remove her to an old woman's home she had refused saying: "I prefer to stay here where all the great men of France are buried. They keep me company. They watch over me."

Lillian was reminded of the talmudic words: "We do not see things as they are, we see them as we are."

Lillian would become so confused by Jay's chaotic living, his dadaism, his contradictions, that she submitted to Djuna's clarifications. Jay's "realism," his need to expose, debunk as he said, his need for reality, did not seem as real as Djuna's intuitive interpretations of their acts.

Lillian had no confidence in herself as a woman. She thought that it was because her father had wanted her to be a boy. She did not see herself as beautiful, and as a girl loved to put on her brother's clothes at first to please her father, and later because it gave her a feeling of strength to take flights from the problems of being a woman. In her brother's jeans, with short hair, with a heavy sweater and tennis shoes, she took on some of her brother's assurance, and reached the conviction that men determined their own destiny and women did not. She chose a man's costume as the primitives chose masks to frighten away the enemy. But the mystery play she had acted was too mysterious. Pretend to be a boy, when what she most wanted was to be loved by one. Act the active lover so the lover will understand she wished him to be active with her. She acted the active lover not because she was the aggressor but because she wanted to demonstrate. . . .

Because her father had wanted her to be a boy she felt she had acquired some masculine traits: courage, activity. When she shifted her ground she felt greater confidence. She thought a woman might love her some day for other qualities as they loved men for their strength, or genius, or wit.

Sabina's appearance, first as a model for Jay's paintings, then more and more into their intimate life, her chaotic and irresistible flow swept Lillian along into what seemed like a passion. But Lillian with Djuna's help, had discovered the real nature of the relationship. It was a desire for an impossible union: she wanted to lose herself in Sabina and BECOME Sabina. This wanting to BE Sabina she had mistaken for love of Sabina's night beauty. She wanted to lie beside her and become her and be one with her and both arise as ONE woman; she wanted to add herself to Sabina, re-enforce the woman in herself, the submerged woman, intensify this woman Lillian she could not liberate fully. She wanted to merge with Sabina's freedom, her capacity for impulsive action, her indifference to consequences. She wanted to smooth her rebellious hair with Sabina's clinging hair, smooth her own denser skin by the touch of Sabina's silkier one, set her own blue eyes on fire from Sabina's

125

fawn eyes, drink Sabina's voice in place of her own, and, disguised as Sabina, out of her own body for good, to become one of the women so loved by her father.

She had loved in Sabina an unborn Lillian. By adding herself to Sabina she would become a more potent woman. In the presence of Sabina she existed more vividly. She chose a body she could love (being critical of her own) a freedom she could obey (which she could never posses) a face she could worship (not being pleased with her own). She believed love quite capable of such metamorphosis.

These feelings had been obscure, unformulated until the night the three of them had gone out together and Sabina had drunk a whole bottle of Pernod. She had become violently ill. Jay and Lillian had nursed her. Sabina was almost delirious. She was easily prone to fever and Lillian was alarmed by the way her face seemed to be consumed from within. She stretched out beside her to watch over her. Jay had gone to sleep in the studio.

In the first version of that night, gathered from Sabina's smoky talk, and Lillian's evasions, Jay had believed that jealousy of him had sprung between them and separated them. But this was only on the surface. Later Lillian saw another drama.

Both Sabina and Lillian, faced with a woman, realized they felt closeness but not desire. They had kissed, and that was all. Sabina wanted something of Lillian: her inexperience, her newness, as if she wanted to begin her own life anew. They both wanted intangible things. Impossible to explain to Jay who made everything so simple, and reduced to acts. He could not understand atmosphere, moods, mysteries.

The true bridge of fascination was the recognition that in Sabina lay a dormant Lillian. A Lillian Jay had not been able to awaken, a liberated Lillian. For he had needed the devoted Lillian.

Sabina was a drought of freedom. Every gesture she

made, every word she uttered. She was free of faithfulness, loyalty, gratitude, devotion, duties, responsibilities, guilts. Even the roles she played were chosen by herself.

Faced with the culmination of their fantasies of a possible closeness to woman, neither one wanted to go further. They both realized the comedy of their pretences. Something so absurd in their bravado towards all experience, in their arrogance about playing Jay's role. They could not escape their femininity, their woman's role, no matter how difficult or complex.

The story which had filtered out had become wrapped in poetry, myth, and drama. It became more and more difficult to reveal the truth, for it was so much more simple, so much more human. Lillian kept the secret because she felt it would make Jay love Sabina more. Jay thought Sabina loved women and that this would explain her water tight compartments.

What would Jay have thought of their hesitations, awkwardnesses, their own bewilderment. He might have laughed at them. They had both played roles. Sabina in a theatrical way, with capes, make up, late arrivals, dramatic effects, disappearances, mysteries. Lillian the one dictated by her outward appearance of naturalness and honesty. "From you I expect honesty," said Jay. Everyone knew Sabina was an actress. Everyone believed Lillian sincere.

Lillian loved Sabina's fluidity, because she wanted it for herself. When she thought she was courting a woman, she was courting Sabina's gift for escape from whatever interrupted the course of passion, whatever interfered with life as an adventure.

They kissed once. It was soft and lovely, but like touching your own flesh. All this was on the edge of their bodies, not at the core. Sabina was touched to see Lillian's bedazzlement. She smiled a triumphant smile.

Lillian had imagined that by loving Sabina a miraculous alchemy would take place. What took place that night was not love of woman. It was a hope of an exchange of selves. It was Sabina's feelings Jay was curious about.

But there were so many things Lillian could not tell Jay. So many things he did not want to hear. Jay thought he could arrive at a dissolution of Sabina's potency by an acid bath of truth. He was seeking to exorcise her power.

He would never believe that they had contemplated allying themselves because they felt incomplete and exposed and less strong than he imagined them. Jay was tone deaf to such secret weaknesses, needs, moments of helplessness.

He would not believe that they both wanted to be consoled as by a sister, or a mother, for his erratic behaviour, his multitude of treacheries.

Antiphonal music of desires at cross currents repeated to infinity. Jay the gate-crasher seeking a truth too black and white. And the key lay in prefabricated myths which appeared in dreams with veiled faces, mute, undecipherable.

Until Djuna took up each strand, delicately separating each one from pain and blindness, the pain of blindness. Strange how in this light, high above the earth, flying through the regions of awareness which Djuna had taken her into by a method of ascension she had finally learned from her. Djuna's words, Djuna the aviator of language, air force for grounded lives.

For a while Lillian had been devoted to both Jay and Sabina. And what had Jay wanted? To own them both? She remembered his letter to her: "You are really strong. I warn you. I am no angel. I am insatiable. I will ask the impossible of you. What it is I don't know."

And a few years later he demanded of her that she understand the presence of Sabina at first only in his paintings, and then later in their lives. He even wanted Lillian to help him know Sabina.

Just before she left Paris for the last time, abdicating, Lillian said to Jay: "Now the time has come for me to tell you of the Sabina I know, because it will make you love her more. You see, what I was given to see was a glimpse of Sabina's innocence. That night . . . we had both dreamed of escaping from our bodies, our moulds. At a certain stage of exaltation all the boundaries are lost, identity too. Sabina was awkward too, she did not know how to behave before a woman. She kept repeating: 'I'd like to be at the beginning of everything, when I could believe, I'd like to be at the beginning of all experience, as you are, able to give yourself, trusting.' She wanted my innocence, and what we want is what we are. And I . . . all my life I could hardly live or breathe for fear of hurting anyone, I had seen Sabina take what she wanted and being loved for it. And I wanted to catch from her by contagion that irresponsibility. Now you will love her more."

"No," said Jay, "much less. Because she would never tell me what you have told me. What you describe—I could not hate that. There's some beauty to it. I have just realized that what I gave you was something coarse and plain compared with that."

"No, Jay, you made me a woman. Sabina would have thrust me back into being a half woman, as I was before I met you."

"Beyond the love," said Jay, "we were friends. Sabina and I will never be friends. I hate her unnecessary complications."

"But they interest you. They are your drugs. I could not give you that. It is I who gave you something plain. I am not a drug."

She looked at the grey blond hair on the nape of his neck, and felt almost capable of staying at his side while he experienced his passion for Sabina. But she was too certain that the body of Sabina would triumph. They were better matched in violence. But what would become of the tender Jay she had known?

So she said: "I must go and see my children. Adele is ill."

"Whatever you do is right. For the first time I see some beauty in it."

The plane was flying into the night now. At times it shivered as from too great an effort to gain altitude.

Jay had been concerned with being the lover of the world, naming all it contained, caressing it with his short and stocky hands, appropriating it, exploring it. And Djuna concerned only with the longitude, and latitude and altitude of human beings in relation to each other.

For a while it seemed as if Lillian were flying into a storm. Luminous signs informed her she must strap herself to her chair. Other passengers slept, confident that strapped to their chairs they would safely reach earth again. Lillian slid the curtain open and through the porthole watched the immensity of space in which sorrows seemed to lose their weight. She looked at the moon, as if to communicate with it, as if it would assure her that the storms of earth could not reach her. Looking at the moon intently it seemed to her that the plane flew more steadily.

It was the year when everyone's attention was focussed on the moon. "The first terrestrial body to be explored will undoubtedly be the moon." Yet how little we know about human beings, thought Lillian. All the telescopes are focussed on the distant. No one is willing to turn his vision inward.

What she had seen of Larry during their marriage was only what he allowed her to see, giant albatross wings, the wings of his goodness. She had been unable to see above or beyond the rim of them. Larry had collaborated in this. He only offered his goodness. He never said: I want, I like, I take but: what do you want? what do you like? He deliberately obscured any vision into his being.

"The moon is the earth's nearest neighbor."

They had slept side by side. In the night, or at dawn, his body had been there. She had felt its radiations. In his voice there were caresses. In his sympathy, a tropical balm.

130

In his goodness, a universe. His attentiveness blinded her. If he had another life, other selves, he turned like a planet, only one face towards Lillian.

"A rocket that would take months to reach one of the planets can travel to the moon in a day or two."

"An instrument station on the moon could communicate with the earth with greater ease than one on Mars or Venus." It was not necessary to circle around Larry or go to Paris, to Mexico. At last she was a receptor for Larry's messages!

"To investigators preoccupied with the remarkable developments in contemporary astronomy and physics the moon had seemed a dead and changeless world."

But only because she had not looked beyond the mask. The rim of density around Larry had been his goodness. It was selfless, almost anonymous. He was present only when summoned, and summoned only by distress. Lillian had fixed the distorted image, but Larry had contributed the mask.

"The moon is an astronomical stone. Because its surface has preserved the record of ancient events, it holds the key to the solar system."

The key to the marriage? Larry had achieved changelessness.

Whereas Lillian was created "out of the air and water that support life on earth which continuously wear away the surface of our planets. Processes in the interior of the earth heave up chains of mountains for demolition by the forces of erosion, and the cycles of building and erosion from one epoch to the next erase the records of the past." That was a portrait of Lillian's turbulences in planetary terms! And of Larry's conservation of the past, of their life together.

"The moon, on the other hand, has neither atmosphere nor oceans, and has never been eroded by wind and water. Furthermore, the circular formations that dominate the moon's topography indicate that its crust has never under-

131

gone the violent changes which are involved in mountain building processes on earth."

Larry had sought to present such an undisturbed surface to Lillian's investigations. But this evenness had been as much a mask as Sabina's more theatrical disguises. What do you feel? Where are you? Will you share my enthusiasms? My friendships?

What had sent Larry so far away from human life into the position of a spectator, so far away from the earth? What had made him wrap himself in an unbreathable atmosphere of selflessness and then be absent from his own body? There were incidents she knew. But she had never coordinated them. She was landing for the first time on this new planet Larry. "In any case, a planet would be cool at birth." His mother had not wanted him to be born. This was the first denial. He had arrived unsummoned by love and jealously resented by his father.

"A cool birth does not exclude the later heating and melting of planetary bodies by radioactive elements they contain."

The child, inhibited by such "a cool birth," sought warmth by running away from home to the huts of the negroes living and working nearby for his father. His father was drilling oil wells in Brazil for an American firm.

His pale mother had faded blue eyes, and wore white dresses which covered her neck and arms, and on which the sewing machine, as if in fear the material would undulate, swell, or fly off like a parachute, had criss-crossed a thousand stitches, tight and overlapping controlling every inch in a stifling design called "shirring."

The father believed in unremitting work, and no idleness or dreaming. He clocked the universe constantly pulling out his watch like a judge at a running match. His mother was beset with fear. Every pleasure was dangerous. Swimming led to drowning, fireworks could blow your finger off, hunting fireflies could anger a rattlesnake, associating with native children would turn you into a "savage."

Larry ran to the negro huts for warmth of voices, warmth of gestures, and warmth of food. He liked the half nakedness, the soft laughter. Home here seemed like a nest, with joyous flesh proximity. Caresses were lavish. There was a hum of content, a hiss of doves. Violence came and went like tropical storms, leaving no traces. (At home a quarrel led to weeks of silence and resentment.) It was Larry's first closeness to human beings. He threw off his too tight clothes. The negro mother was his nurse. She smiled upon his fairness. Her flowered cotton dress smelled of spices, and she moved as easily as cotton tree seeds. When she was happy her body undulated with laughter. Their laundry, swollen like sail boats, was more vivid than a rainbow.

Yet she betrayed him.

He had played with the naked dark children. After swimming in all the forbidden lagoons and rivers, they had openly admired each other, half mocking, half tender. In his own home Larry had wanted to repeat these games with his younger brother. But it was not a swimming adventure as it was out in the country, among plants and grass and reeds. It was in the bathroom. Larry thought all discoveries of bodies could be made as merrily as by the riverside. His younger brother was so delicate, his hair so fragile, his skin like a girl's. With delight they contrasted skin tones, breadth of chest, length of legs, strength of legs. But this scientific erotic exploration was watched by the nurse through the transom window, and the same thing she laughed at in nature, she now reported like a policeman on the frontier of some forbidden land.

A shocking treachery from the world he loved with a trusting passion, a treachery which came not from where he might have expected it, the shaggy browed father with his eyes too deeply set in tired flesh, or from the cool eyes of the pale mother, but from the spice-scented, barefooted, tenderhanded black mother he loved. Such treacheries throw human beings into outer space, at a safe distance from human beings. They are propelled into space by attacks from the human specie. Could not the nurse have laughed at the children exploring the wonders of the body? Could she not have laughed at their games as she laughed at their games while swimming? Did she not herself keep her warm dry hand on his coltish shoulder blades and comb his hair with her fingers "To feel the silk of it"? He had almost reached the earth with her, with her he had almost been born fully to his molten life.

The child has set his planet's course, has chosen his place in outer space, according to the waves of hostility or fear he had encountered. Pain was the instrument which set him afloat and determined his course. The sun, whether gold, white, or black, having failed him he will exist henceforward in a more temperate zone, twilit ones, less exposed to danger.

Lillian had at first misinterpreted his silences. He communicated only with children, and with animals. His absences (if only I knew where he was when he was gone) distressed her. Never knowing until later that, as a measure of safety he had sought the periphery, the region of no-pain, where human beings could not reach him.

The first betrayal had thrust him into space to rotate at a certain distance from the source and origin of the first collision.

Lillian calculated the effect of his not having been wanted. The effect of adopting a family and then being betrayed. The atmosphere of gaiety and freedom was altered. When the negro shack was accidentally destroyed by fire he had no regrets. When he was made to sail away from the Brazilian planet to England, he was sullen. The parents had decided he could not grow up into a native "savage." He needed discipline. Larry already preferred drumming to

134

sixteenth-century English songs. He liked the stamping of bare feet more than the waltzing of high heels and patent leather shoes. He liked vivid pinks, not his mother's colorless dresses. He liked time for dreaming, not his father's tightly filled days.

He entered a cold atmosphere of discipline and puritanism. His mother's sister held the watch now, and also a whip. Every infraction was severely punished. The long walk to school was timed. The purchase of a water pistol was a crime. Pulling a little girl's hair or pushing her down on the grass was a crime. And as for the mystery of where her legs started and asking if inside the bouffant dress there was a corolla as in the heart of a poppy. . . . Whatever food she served had no taste, because she imposed it. She measured and enforced time and appetite, just as she commanded the flowers to bloom at a certain date.

Larry disappeared behind a façade of obedience. There was a Sea of Tranquility on the moon. Larry lived there. There were no ruffles on the surface. Outwardly he conformed until his marriage to Lillian. Lillian having spent her childhood in Mexico, seemed to be a messenger from the happier days of Brazil.

"The relative smoothness of the lunar surface poses a question."

Much of men's energies were being spent on such questions, Lillian's on the formation of Larry's character. Their minds were fixed on space; hers on the convolutions of Larry's feelings.

Her vehement presence became the magnet. She summoned him back from solitude. She was curious about his feelings, about his silences, about his retractions. His mother's first wish that he should not exist at all was pitted against Lillian's wish that he exist in a more vivid and heightened way. She made a game of his retreats, pretended to discover his "caves." He was truly born in her warmth and her conviction of his existence.

How slender was the form he offered to the world's vision, how slender a slice of his self, a thin sliver of an eighth of the moon on certain nights. She was not deceived as to the dangers of another eclipse. She could hear, as you hear in musique concrete, the echo in vast space which corresponds to new dimensions in science, the echo which was never heard in classical music.

Lillian felt that in the husband playing the role of husband, in the scientist playing his role of scientist, in the father playing his role of father, there was always the danger of detachment. He had to be maintained on the ground, given a body. She breathed, laughed, stirred, and was tumultuous for him. Together they moved as one living body and Larry was passionately willed into being born, this time permanently. Larry, Larry, what can I bring you? Intimacy with the world? She was on intimate terms with the world. While he maintained a world in which Lillian was the only inhabitant, or at least the reigning one.

Such obsession with reaching the moon, because they had failed to reach each other, each a solitary planet! In silence, in mystery, a human being was formed, was exploded, was struck by other passing bodies, was burned, was deserted. And then it was born in the molten love of the one who cared.

AFTERWORD

The Two Faces of Death
in Anais Nin's
Seduction of The Minotaur

*They awaken, to become guardians of all the living and
the dead.*   Heraclitus

In what Jung called the process of individuation there comes
the moment, crucial, heightened with archetypical significance,
of the meeting with the minotaur of one s own self, the minotaur
whose foreboding countenance we spend so much of our days,
and nights, avoiding as if to face it would bring instantaneous
and total dispersion, oblivion. Yet as awareness grows and the
face remains unseen we are seized by the certain knowledge that
everything depends on removing the veil, a knowledge we would
like to relegate to the vague and uncertain realm of suspicion,
hunch, where it might easily be dismissed so that we might be
free to "do other things," "get on with living." And it is at such a
point that the suspicion takes other forms: perhaps there is no
life, without this encounter which we avoid; perhaps we are all
dead here, until we look into the face which alone can waken us.
Life seems to expand, and we become conscious that the point
which we occupy might constitute only a narrow corner from
which we fearfully project what might be but parcels of the self
into a future whose rigid, unmoving, Parmenidean constrictions
serve to stifle and to kill. There is that within us which wants us
to expand with the flow of life, to occupy points ever farther
removed from the quiet center of the vortex of living, to become
flowing selves, free and at home with our essential condition.

Anais Nin has written about the growth of awareness of a
woman, Lillian, who as a result of her journeys into the cities of
the interior (a phrase which forms the title of Nin's "continuous
novel") has begun the journey homeward. Many journeys, one
journey.

Seduction of The Minotaur, like all of Nin's novels, touches reverberations in us, sometimes of themes long familiar, problems long since met and solved, sometimes of those as yet unannounced themes the import of which still escapes us, themes which we yet clearly anticipate. She who has been there, where we have been, and she who has been there before us, where, we suspect, we must go if we are to continue the journey, she who holds the golden thread, she leads the way. That is to say, the novel has something to teach. As do all of Nin's novels. Their resonance in life must be charted at depths to which few novels reach. That is to say, the novel is difficult. As are all of Nin's novels. It is a novel which requires not merely reading, but meditating, or, to use a most exact word here, reflecting.

To read Nin's novels, one must become reflective. The femininity of this author has been universally acknowledged. Everyone has said it, in one way or another: "Nin is a woman." Henry Miller. William Carlos Williams. Lawrence Durrell. *The New York Times.* Even a scientist at Stanford. This "feminine touch in the arts," as William Carlos Williams called it, is not something which, like truth, loves to hide! But what does it mean? What about the men who read Nin? What might they need to know about how to read her, given the fact that it is woman writing? "It's disturbing, it forces a man to an opposite extreme," said William Carlos Williams, of the feminine touch in Nin's work.

It would be terribly easy—and dangerous—for the mind to begin playing games at this point. But what if it were already too late for playing games? What then?

First of all, one must beware: not every woman who writes has this feminine touch. Unfortunately, however, all the comments made by all the men about femininity in art are posed in such a way as to propagate such a fiction. The fact is otherwise: this so-called feminine touch is a rare quality, found in so few writers that the possession of it by one, Anais Nin, is alone enough to distinguish her as among the very finest, subtlest, most acute sensibilities in recent literature. The possession of this quality is a rare gift. Should we not, then, consider ourselves responsible for a more honest articulation of its defining properties than is conveyed by the vague term "feminine touch"?

If it were a matter of a "feminine touch" alone, all women writers would convey what Nin conveys. Not so. Her vision is distinguished, and even in ways unique. Her metaphysic reveals a particular point of departure, a place from which the voice of this extraordinary woman and novelist speaks to us in such a way as to invite our reflection. For it immediately strikes an attentive reader of Nin's books: here is a world I would do well to enter, a world rich in promise of insights, revelations, perhaps the golden thread itself, leading to the very center of the labyrinth.

But there is difficulty at the beginning. ("It's disturbing," said William Carlos Williams). One suspects very early in his explorations of the world of Anais Nin that it is one difficult to know, that to read the novel *Seduction of The Minotaur* without somehow encountering one's own shadowy self at the center of one's own labyrinth is not to have read the book. The path to the book ought to be well-marked: "Danger" "Not For Everyone" "For Lovers of Self-Knowledge Only, If Any There Be" "Magic Theatre". For just as in Hesse's *Steppenwolf* there is a magic theatre containing all the doors to the self, doors opening onto archetype after archetype, so in the magic theatre of the world of Nin's fiction (where everyday reality is infused with the glow and "patina," to use one of the novelist's favorite words, of symbolical transformation) one finds himself face to face with the mythical proportions of the everyday and the near-at-hand. It does not take much exposure to this world to begin to suspect that here nothing is absent, nothing avoided, that somehow the theme is life itself, far beyond any "feminine touch." Life itself, seen through the eyes of woman. Yes. That is more like it.

Increasingly, then, as one reflects on the world of Anais Nin, he begins to see that openness to that world is prerequisite to entering it. It is the world of woman, yes. But not only that. It is the world of woman's wisdom. She has offered it to us, the

139

woman of clear insight, clairvoyance, the artist, the maker of illusions. This distinguishes her. One cannot insist too strongly on that.

The feminine touch which truly disturbs, disturbs in the creative sense, which urges toward openness, expansion, insight, entry into the Heraclitean fire of nature and life, that indeed is present in all of Nin's work. "It forces a man to an opposite extreme," said William Carlos Williams. Yes. Toward the anima. As though Nin's success as an artist were proven by the effect her work has on the psyche. The Literature of Bread: all of Nin's work belongs to this genre, as yet an uncatalogued company. Perhaps never before in the history of literature has the anima been so conscious of itself as it is in the works of Anais Nin: a consciousness which belies the presence of animus at the very core of the being—so that within the work one feels the most compelling evidence of the reality of that toward which those who strive do indeed strive: precisely that totality of being which is the end toward which the process of individuation tends as towards a fate. Caught up in the dynamics of this process, the individual who happens to have the good fortune to come upon the door to the world of Nin's work will immediately recognize within a clearly articulated image of that process a body of work which provides an enlightening guide to those cities of the interior through which he himself will have been traveling. This will, of course, be an exciting moment in his life. Even if disturbing.

Nin's work has recently gained a careful, a concernful audience among the young. She has virtually become the Princess of the young, much as Cocteau at another time and for different reasons was the Prince of the young, and indeed in many ways still is. That audience comprising those who read Hesse, consult the I Ching, search for meaning and truth (to use the old-fashioned words), those who are listening to Indian music and the soundless sound of OM, those chanting mantras, those many who are seriously studying oriental philosophies, that is, increasingly more of the young, are also turning toward the work of the writers who know. (Wisdom—that attentive and receptive activity of giving heed to the nature of things—stands apart, said Heraclitus, from all else.) This increasing audience is simply the latest addition to Nin's previous one, but it is a significant addition: there seems now to be an intense awareness of the crucial importance of awareness. And Nin is above all aware.

Anais Nin, like everyone else who writes, has two kinds of readers: those who are searching, and those highly skilled in traveling the labyrinthine roads of the cities of the interior, deep-sea divers, old salts. In *The Novel of The Future* Anais Nin confides that she has a whole trunk full of letters from those who have said, "You are writing my diary." Those would be the searchers, I suppose. The old salts would know that she is writing her own diary, which is my diary, your diary, his diary, everyone's diary. A man at home with the Upanishads, with the Koan approach to awareness, with Nietzsche, with Jung—he will readily enter the world of Anais Nin. He will know, surely, its vastness soon after he enters. "This is no small world," he will be obliged to say. "In it, one must spend much time—before its dimensions begin to reveal themselves, vast dimensions, perhaps illimitable." To say that is to say something which distinguishes a work. This is no mere matter of a "feminine touch," a phrase which begins to sound more than ridiculous at this point.

THE GOLDEN THREAD

> Some voyages have their inception in the blueprint of a dream, some in the urgency of contradicting a dream. Lillian's recurrent dream of a ship that could not reach the water, that sailed laboriously, pushed by her with great effort, through city streets, had determined her course toward the sea, as if she would give this ship, once and for all, its proper sea bed. (5)

A magnificent opening! We are in the heart of the myth. ("Proceed from the dream outward," said Jung.) There is the sense of wonder which comes from closeness to the elements. Something momentous is about to occur, a breakthrough.

> She had landed in the city of Golconda, where the sun painted everything with gold, the lining of her thoughts, the

worn valises, the plain beetles, Golconda of the golden age, the golden aster, the golden eagle, the golden goose, the golden fleece, the golden robin, the golden-rod, the golden seal, the golden warbler, the golden wattles, the golden wedding, and the gold fish, and the gold of pleasure, the goldstone, the gold thread, the fool's gold. (5)

Taste that prose! If ever prose tasted good, really good, this must be it. Wattles, warblers, weddings—all suffused with gold. What can this mean? There is something vulgar in talking about symbols.

The visionary artist doesn't merely use symbols. He sees that they are there. His seeing is itself in essence symbolic transformation, and he knows this as his point of departure, it being that which gives his work life. He sees that things are golden, and so they are.

Lillian has come to Golconda to escape. She, fugitive from herself, would like to burrow into forgetfulness. Yet here fate (yes, fate—as though at times things are decided for us) is to meet the golden illumination of Golconda, and through her very first encounter there its human counterpart: the wise, visionary, illuminating, clairvoyant Dr. Hernandez. He is marked for death, and this fact touches him profoundly. It is that which does not allow him to join the games which the others play. It is that which dictates his truth and his concern. It opens him, this death (has he chosen his death, could he not have escaped it?), for deep encounter. But as Lillian will later have reason to see, he has not been fully opened, he has lived with more caution than one would have thought necessary or proper for a man living so close to the realization of our mortality:

> He had something to say, which he had not said, and he had left taking with him his secrets.
> If only Dr. Hernandez had not postponed that deeper, wilder talk which ran underground through the myths of dreams, shouted through architectural crevices, screamed eloquently through the eyes of statues, from the depths of all the ancient cities within ourselves, if he had not merely signaled distress like a deaf-mute . . . . if only awareness had

142

not appeared through the interstices of memory, between bars of light and bars of shadows...if only human beings did not draw the blinds, don disguises, and live in isolation cells marked: not yet time for revelations... (94-95)

Yet it is this powerful passage of regret for things unsaid which leads directly to the magnificent moment of effective discovery: "Lillian was journeying homeward." There is an aesthetic swing here in the novel, impossible to convey, where the poetry of revelation and the music of the prose come together in a rhythmic pulsation wholly appropriate to the dramatic and psychological situation, and Lillian is borne forth toward the future on a wave whose force is brilliantly conveyed by the chemistry of art. We experience directly the fact of her growth, and because the art is finely wrought, the experience is an exciting one. Anais Nin, not unlike her own character Dr. Hernandez, issues, through her work, compelling invitations to live differently, more fully, more flowingly. This is not to say she is a moralist; it is to say that she is an artist, one of the rare artists whose work it has been to fashion a literature of bread, a work which feeds the soul (let us allow ourselves the old-fashioned word, for the word psyche seems to resist flow).

Our criticism does not allow a grouping of works into anything like a literature of bread. That is a pity, for if it were possible so to place a work, we would have gone some way toward defining the crucial importance of Anais Nin, in simply placing her work there. Many correlations would be seen directly which otherwise would, as is indeed the case, have been invisible and therefore in need of explanation. What we need is some kind of explanatory principle, akin to the notion of a bead game in Hesse's fiction, which would, by placing Nin where she truly is, show us who her companions in art and in life are. Hesse did this for himself, choosing those companions whom we meet in *Magister Ludi, Journey To The East,* and *Steppenwolf:* Goethe, Albertus Magnus, Paul Klee, Mozart, Schubert, the I Ching, Pablo the drug user, St. Thomas Aquinas. And into this magic circle steps Anais Nin. There is much more than a "feminine

143

touch in the arts" at work here. Her readers have placed her in a very special circle, the circle of magicians.

> Henry has fallen under the spell of a remarkable old man who is fantastic and psychic, a painter gone mad in Zurich, who talks in symbols. When this old man Crowley met me he refused to look at me. He said I was a mystic, all light, thousands of years old, that I ensorcelled men's souls and that he did not dare look into my eyes.[1]

Perhaps the old man was right. In any case, he saw the light and the wisdom ("thousands of years old") without reading the books (then, of course, mostly unwritten) and that is more than one can say for the more myopic of the literary critics, those who fail to see that the artist, too, incarnates spirit. Our age has forgotten this, the ancient and indeed sacred role of the artist, who brings us the bread which nourishes and sustains, the bread which is the wafer, the symbol, the cipher, that which we absolutely require if we are not to be lost in the ever expanding regions of the space which life reveals to us as we move on toward the ultimate dispersion, that which perhaps has spoken to us haltingly in natural phenomena, as wind over water, that which speaks to us so clearly in the work of Anais Nin.

The artist, too, incarnates spirit. It bears repeating. Our age has forgotten this— has chosen to forget it, one is almost tempted to say— and thus the lack of energy, the lack of a real aristocracy of art, the lack of a metaphysical and psychological literature which I have called the literature of bread. But Nin is the princess of the young—showing the way—and one of the miracles is that she is of our age, our tired age which has produced more trash and taken it more seriously than any other age in the history of man.

THE ENCOUNTER

There were tears in Lillian's eyes, for having made friends immediately not with a new, a beautiful, a drugging place, but

---

[1]February, 1934, *Unpublished Selections from The Diary,* The Duane Schneider Press, Athens, Ohio, 1968.

with a man intent on penetrating the mysteries of the human labyrinth from which she was a fugitive. (19)

It is Dr. Hernandez, marked for deep encounter, he who investigates in his laboratories the ancient Indian drugs of remembrance (Pablo, of Hesse's *Steppenwolf*), he who controls the traffic in the drugs of forgetfulness (he has enemies, mortal enemies), he who is called "The Lie Detector" in *A Spy In The House of Love,* and perhaps the modern Christ in *House of Incest.* "He was suffering and it was this which made him so aware of others' difficulties." (21) Lillian has come to Golconda to forget, but she encounters Dr. Hernandez, and sees that there is too much light for forgetfulness. She has arrived at her destination, only to see that the journey has just begun. But it does not really begin, not the swing homeward, the real entry into Heraclitean fire, until the death of Dr. Hernandez. "Lillian could not believe in the Doctor's death." (93) A death impossible to believe. The modern Christ. Only in the refusal to accept death, even in the very face of the most brutally telling facts, does Lillian begin to move toward the minotaur. The passage in which this movement is traced is one of such beauty, and such power, that it must be quoted in full here.

> Lillian did not believe in the death of Doctor Hernandez, and yet she heard the shot, she felt in her body the sound of the car hitting the pole, she knew the moment of death, as if all of them had happened to her.
> He had something to say, which he had not said, and he had left taking with him his secrets.
> If only Doctor Hernandez had not postponed that deeper, wilder talk which ran underground through the myths of dreams, shouted through architectural crevices, screamed eloquently through the eyes of statues, from the depths of all the ancient cities within ourselves, if he had not merely signaled distress like a deaf mute..............if only awareness had not appeared through the interstices of memory, between bars of lights and bars of shadows...if only human beings did not draw the blinds, don disguises, and live in isolation cells marked: not yet time for revelations...
> ...if only they had gone down together, down the caverns

145

of the soul with picks, lanterns, cords, oxygen, X-rays, food, following the blueprints of all the messages from the geological depths where lay hidden the imprisoned self....

According to the definition, tropic meant a turning and changing, and with the tropics Lillian turned and changed, and she swung between the drug of forgetfulness and the drug of awareness, as the natives swung in their hammocks, as the jazz players swung into their rhythms, as the sea swung in its bed

turned
changed

Lillian was journeying homeward. (94-95)

After this passage, Lillian moves out of the present of Golconda, backward into the deep abysm of her past, forward into a future where she will be able to see things, as though for the first time, with her own eyes. She has climbed the ladder to fire, has touched the fiery center, has descended into the labyrinth even with the golden thread of her inability to believe in the death of Doctor Hernandez, has met the minotaur, has come through:

Lillian was journeying homeward. The detours of the labyrinth did not expose disillusion, but unexplored dimensions. Archeologists of the soul never returned empty handed. Lillian had felt the existence of the labyrinth beneath her feet like the excavated passageways under Mexico City, but she had feared entering it and meeting the Minotaur who would devour her.

Yet now that she had come face to face with it, the Minotaur resembled someone she knew. It was not a monster. It was a reflection upon a mirror, a masked woman, Lillian herself, the hidden masked part of herself unknown to her, who had ruled her acts. She extended her hand toward this tyrant who could no longer harm her. It lay upon the mirror of the plane's round portholes, traveling through the clouds, a fleeting face, her own face, clear and definable only when darkness came. (111)

It was Heraclitus, master of clear obscurity, who first articulated the premise that it is in changing that things find repose. This is something we hear directly in music, where eternity and the transitory become one in the most illogical, improbable and yet totally compelling union of opposites. *Seduction of The Minotaur* ought to be read, at least on one of its many levels, as music. Then we would understand readily enough the dynamic peace which pervades the glorious ending of the book, not a peace without strife (the common condition is strife, said Heraclitus, without which nothing would be) but a passionate serenity, a belief in the richness of life, a fullness, an illumination, a fire, gold.

The death of Doctor Hernandez has been the death which brings life, and Lillian is Lazarus, come back from the dead with a new and keen awareness of our mortality and thus of our vividity. About this return there is great sadness ("Jesus wept.") but no morbidity. Lillian is alive when she leaves Golconda, and we, who have been with her on her journey into the cities of the interior, are disposed toward her with a trust in her capacity to remain alive, even to bring others to life through awareness.

As though to balance the light which suffuses this book, at the very core the novelist has let fall over the structure the shadow of death, not a death in which it is not possible to believe but a death of living, palpable, black, silent, ominous, sterile presence.

In the middle of a party on a Mexican general's yacht, in the middle of the fireworks of illusion, the comet tails showering light on the water, Lillian meets a young man, Michael Lomax, and confides in him: "Every now and then, at a party, in the middle of living, I get this feeling that I have slipped off." (59) And he answers, "I have that feeling all the time, not now and then." (59) He invites Lillian to his house, in an ancient city, and she travels with him through the night, through the valley of the shadow of death, into the ancient city, into the heart of darkness, death itself. Here she finds ruins, silence, muted streets, vultures, but no singing birds, and no wind. Even the fireworks here have an aura of desperation, and the children fling themselves under the showers of gold, as if to take upon themselves the momentary promise of life which the dispersing intensity seems to offer, but in vain. Here, Michael is king of all the dead,

147

but he has no subjects, for the dead do not exist at all, not at all. They who do not move, do not exist. This is not the death of Doctor Hernandez, who set in motion the wheel of the dharma. Perhaps in the case of Doctor Hernandez, there is no death. One would do well here to reflect on the meaning which so clearly strikes home in the last pages of Tolstoy's "The Death of Ivan Ilych." Not that Doctor Hernandez is Ivan Ilych! No, nothing like that is meant. Rather, what is being suggested is the genesis of the book, *Seduction of The Minotaur,* itself. Why not come right out and say it? Anais Nin as bodhisattva! Perhaps that would be a bit crude, after all.

For what we see when we look behind the book, to the artist, this artist who possesses a certain "feminine touch," to use that phrase again, is not precisely she who sees clearly that what people need, absolutely need, more than anything else perhaps, is the transfiguration of things, transmogrification, transcendence, transformation, the artist transpiring (wonderful word!) to transmit the truth if not the fact, death and transfiguration. And so Anais Nin shows us the two faces of death.

Michael is a fool: time's fool, and his homosexuality is but one manifestation of his more fundamental fleeing from the truth of his own being as incarnate. To Lillian he has said: "All I ask, since I can't keep you here, is that in your next incarnation you be born a boy, and then I will love you." (67) Not being able to live within the real channels of his present incarnation, he lives within the dream channels of a world without women. Could Michael Lomax be saved through awareness? The answer to that would be another novel, and, of necessity, a seduction of the minotaur. But for the present novel, as for the present life, Lillian has no choice but to leave him in hell with his dream, which is death. He has refused the gift of presence. While present, he is absent, even as in his city, the city of the dead, there are tolling church bells without ritual:

> The church bells tolled persistently although there was no ritual to be attended, as if calling day and night to the natives buried by the volcano's eruption years before. (60)

148

Has any philosopher ever defined the real as that which is truly capable of receiving love?

It was St. John of the Cross who said, "Where you do not find love, put love, and there you will find it." Yet everything would seem—would it not?—to depend on receptivity. The valley of some dreams is not receptive to love.

Michael's dream is of that which cannot be realized. It is the dream of death. Lillian says, "But not to feel . . . not to love . . . is like dying within life, Michael." Precisely, Anais Nin has shown us the two faces of death. That has been the place within the form of this book of this shadow of death which falls in its midst, reminding us that the lights of the carnival which dominate the book's many scapes are transitory, fleeing, fleeting, fire. The author's compassion touches Michael as it touches and illumines all her characters—as though to know precisely where a character is is thereby to create him in compassion—but her vision is too clear, and she sees far too much, to allow her to tell anything but the truth. If the truth is devastating, it is devastating. Sympathy has nothing to do with it. As far as the vision of this particular book extends, Michael is lost. But Anais Nin's world is in the deepest sense one which nourishes hope. There is no finality, no system, no judge, no absolute. There is the river, the flow, and always the possibility of encounter. Such an encounter as between Lillian and Doctor Hernandez. Michael Lomax might in another context emerge as Lazarus, wakened from the sleep of death. Wakened, drawn from absence into the epiphany of presence itself, unadorned and irrevocably real.

WIND OVER WATER: AN IMAGE OF DISPERSION

In the ancient city of the interior where Michael Lomax dwells with his dream of an impossible, an unreal, world, there is no wind, no wind which moves, which animates, which gives life that exists only in the act of constant dispersion. Michael wants eternity, a frozen world from which the mischievous work of the womb will have been banned, a world where Eve stands frozen in the snow. Eve is never frozen. Nietzsche knew it well,

149

for he asked, "What if truth were a woman, what then?" What then? Heraclitus, in a word. The river, the moving water which is fire. Water in communion with wind—dispersion, life itself, flux, change, chance, epiphany, flow. A world where fire and water do not combat each other.[2] The union of opposites. The magic circle of yin and yang. Love, and bread.

But there is water, even as the book began with a thrust toward water. There are fountains playing on the terraces of that ancient city, yet they seem akin to the stone statue in *Don Giovanni* whose voice echoes from the hollow realm of shades, and what it says is Death.

With one of those quick transitions of which she is a master, Anais Nin brings us out of this valley of shades into the dazzling light of Lillian's new life, there where she has reached that point from which it is possible for her to look backward into the abyss of time which we call the past, there to see the receding distances, the muted cries of regretted acts, the dead loves, the things which, though remembered with what exquisite care, have receded utterly into oblivion. It is then that she sees that time does not recede in two directions, but only in one, the direction of the past, and that what seems to lie before her is something which men have been compelled to call the eternal return. Everything returns. It was Doctor Hernandez who said that to Lillian:

> And one day we open our eyes, and there we are caught in the same pattern, repeating the same story. How could it be otherwise? The design comes from within us. It is internal. (19)

And at that moment, he gave her a key to the labyrinth. The face of the Minotaur was her own face, hidden in the shades of what the Vedantins have so accurately termed avidya, unawareness. Doctor Hernandez was awake, he was wise. It was his death in which Lillian could not believe.

"Lillian was journeying homeward." (95) She had begun to accept the gift of presence, the immensity of the *persona*, the

---

[2]In the language of the Crow Indians of Montana, the same word is used to designate both fire and water. The meaning must be taken from the context.

heraldic proportions of things, events, relations. Life moves out of the picture frame, ceases to be one-dimensional, begins to astonish even where one would expect never to find the astonishing, even in the most humble, everyday reality:

> It was as if having begun to see the true Doctor Hernandez, solitary, estranged from his wife and his children by her jealousy and hatred of Golconda immersed only in the troubled, tragic life of a pleasure city, she could also see for the first time, around the one dimensional profile of her husband, a husband leaving for work, a father bending over his children, an immense new personality. (98)

And not only does Lillian begin to see the vastness of the face of her husband, she begins to see his face in other faces, that in freeing a prisoner who was a stranger she had in reality been freeing a prisoner who was her husband, that we are all prisoners whose freedom, if realized, would never cease to astonish, never cease to nourish, never cease to grow and to create. Yes, she is on her way, homeward:

> Sudden death had exposed the preciousness of human love and human life. All the negations, withdrawals, indifferences seemed like the precursors of absolute death, and were to be condemned. (103)

Camus said that we must imagine Sisyphus happy. Lillian is journeying homeward, perhaps even to teach her children to wipe the crumbs off the table. Perhaps to remember a black dog which, having eaten a piece of newly baked bread, had crumbs scattered like stars on his snout. For on the journey homeward Lillian remembers. We could say that this remembering is all a part of the process of individuation, or we could simply see it as part of the poetry of living with one's own eyes open. Remember to remember. Here are we again, as we always were, in the cities of the interior, where dwell the archetypes, the hidden faces, the fatalities which we seem bound to repeat. Prospero, with what an informed love for his daughter Miranda, bids her remember, remember. Forgetfulness is misery, condemnation to abysmal repetition. Wakefulness is reality, even moksha, release.

151

In form, *Seduction of The Minotaur* is a perfect Sonata, in three movements: Allegro vivace; Largo, con molto affeto; Rondo, Allegro. The Largo movement is comprised of the dark, somber section on Michael Lomax. All else is the rondo, the round, the ever-recurring, the common ground of walking into joy—and we are left imagining Sisyphus happy. "Never separate depth from form," a friend said to me. "Say that, but do not use the word depth and do not use the word form," I said to him. "Art in service of release," he answered, with what a marvelous directness I had thought then.

WAYNE MCEVILLY

This Afterword originally appeared as an article in the *New Mexico Quarterly*, Winter-Spring 1969.